My name is
Happiness

My name is Happiness

Veronica Plumbe

BROWN
DOG
BOOKS

Published under licence by Brown Dog Books and The Self-Publishing Partnership, 7 Green Park Station, Bath BA1 1JB

www.selfpublishingpartnership.co.uk

ISBN printed book: 978-1-78545-359-5

Cover design by Andrew Prescott
Internal design by Andrew Easton

This book is printed on FSC certified paper

Printed and bound in the UK

Acknowledgements

I would like to thank Simon Porter, M.D. of Duroc Media, for introducing me to Georgina Lamb and Melanie Shepherd of the David Shepherd Wildlife Foundation and, in turn, thank them for their wonderful support and encouragement.

Also Andrew, Olivia and Edmund for their undying patience, boggling technical support and heroic conservation enthusiasm.

Foreword

The themes of wildlife, family and friendship provide the vital ingredients for a wonderfully captivating and educational read, which introduces young audiences to the importance of conservation.

With its beautiful and playful visuals, this charming book immediately transports the reader to the wild plains of Africa, following the courageous character of 'Happiness' the warthog. From the very first page to the last lines, I was absorbed with this enchanting and heartfelt story.

Veronica is a long-time friend and supporter of the David Shepherd Wildlife Foundation, a charity built on a heritage of using creative art as a tool for education and change. We firmly believe that the future health of our planet and all living things rests with today's children. If we can help develop, inspire and encourage an interest in the natural world then we will have achieved our aim, and this moving story continues that concept, through the wonderful words of 'My Name is Happiness'.

I hope you enjoy this magical book as much as I did!

Georgina Lamb –
Head of Programmes and Policy
David Shepherd Wildlife Foundation

www.davidshepherd.org
@DSWFWildlife

Contents

Part I

Happiness Makes New Friends

Chapter 1

The Incident with Truffle

Happiness

My name is Happiness

My name is Happiness Hazel Horner, Happy for short, and I am a warthog piglet. My parents named me Happiness because I smiled the very moment I was born.

I was born on the Gorogoro Game Reserve in Africa nearly two years ago. Until recently I lived in a den with my sounder: my grandparents, Grandma and Grandpa (who are too old to live alone any more), my mother Mama, my brothers Quiver and Truffle, and my little sister Winkle. My father, Papa, lives in a different den, which is normal for male warthogs, and visits Mama's den from time to time to warn her if he has spotted any predators lurking around.

My father is strong and handsome with lots of knobbly warts and powerful tusks, while my mother is very pretty, with soft, chocolate brown eyes that sparkle in the African sun. Mama's den is close to a watering hole so Papa dug us a mud bath to roll in, which helps keep the flies off our skin.

During the day we would dig or forage for food, play chase and explore. We always made time to attend our grandparents' school on Sunday mornings, though.

Life was good, but one day our happy routine was suddenly disrupted by an incident that would change my life forever.

We were always told that we had to be on the lookout for predators such as hyenas, leopards and lions, but I now know that there is a far worse killer out on the plains of Africa, and that, I'm afraid, is poachers.

If you've ever been to my part of the world, you will know just how hot and dry it gets here, but for those of you who haven't, I can assure you that in November, when the incident happened, it was most uncomfortable. Grit coated my skin and my eyelashes, and our waterhole and mud bath had completely dried up. Just thinking about it makes me itch all over.

Grandpa described that particular day as "a real scorcher and hot enough to grill a burger on the back of a buffalo's bottom"!

Winkle was so hot she begged Mama to let her go down to the river for a swim. "Please, please, Mama," she whined, stamping her little trotter. "I'm so hot and thirsty!"

Mama eventually gave in. "Alright, we'll go but we must keep our eyes peeled for danger. Everyone's boiling and we desperately need water. It's your turn to be lookout," she ordered, fixing me with her loving eyes. "No daydreaming, Happiness."

Generally, we took turns to be on watch and had family rules that were never to be broken. For example, if one of us was attacked, then the rest had to run, no matter what. Only my father was strong enough to take on a predator, so there was no point in any of the rest of us sticking around.

Since my grandparents were staying at home to rest, I promised to bring some water back for them. I rubbed snouts with my grandparents, picked up the water pouch that my friends – the local tribesmen – had given me, clenched it firmly between my teeth and scampered outside to join the others in the dazzling sunshine.

"See if you can spot the little five," suggested Grandma. "You can teach the others all about them at our Sunday school."

I nodded keenly.

We tiptoed cautiously along the well-worn track, quiet as mice; even the sound of a single twig snapping could carry far through the still air and alert predators to our presence. Being warthogs, we are considered a tasty snack for a rumbling stomach, but I had no desire to become a meal for anyone.

Winkle

The ground was so hot, and we ran quickly from one shaded spot to another, always checking that the coast was clear before moving on. Truffle, Quiver and Winkle played hide-and-seek along the way, but I preferred to have a jolly good sniff at the huge piles of elephant dung or to press my snout deep into the neat, round nuggets deposited along the path by gazelles and kudus; the distinctive, glossy blue-black wildebeest droppings were fun to roll with my snout.

Taking a deep breath, I filled my nostrils with these delicious aromas, soon becoming lost in my own dreamy thoughts of the river. I hoped it would be just like the last time we went down there when the plant life had all joined together to become a huge, floating lilo. It had been so dense and buoyant that I climbed aboard some cabbage leaves, tied a long tree-creeper to my ankle so I wouldn't drift away, and lay on my back to dream with my trotters pointing up into the air. Just thinking about it made me giggle out loud.

"Sshhh," hushed Mama, "concentrate!"

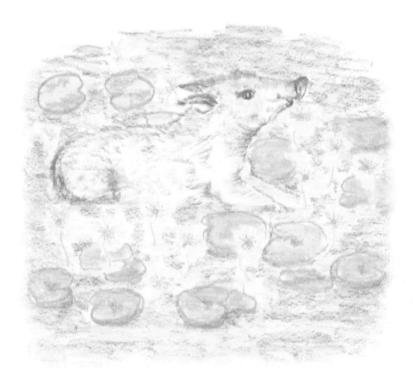

"Sorry," I whispered, looking around me. I pricked up my ears and sniffed deeply. The tall grasses were motionless; the coast seemed clear so I decided to have a quick look for the *little five* as Grandma had suggested. They are inspired by the African *big five*, which you may have heard of: lion, elephant, leopard, rhino and buffalo.

It didn't take me long. Two 'rhino beetles' had locked horns, getting ready for battle over a bashful female who watched quietly from the sidelines. An 'ant lion' dug determinedly into the ground, accidentally chucking crumbs of soil into my face as he went about his work, and a tiny 'elephant shrew' ran over my foot. A pair of 'buffalo weaver' birds sat side by side in the tree above me, looking down as we walked past.

"Have you seen any hungry leopards or lions about?" I asked them.

They shook their heads so I went back to my game. Now I just had the 'leopard tortoise' left to spot.

"Happiness," whispered Mama, "I must dig up some bulbs for tea. Ask Truffle to come and help me; his tusks are nice and strong."

But Truffle had smelled something and was already on his knees digging hard into the ground right in the middle of a clearing – in full view of any predators!

"Truffle, Mama needs you!" I hissed, trying to get his attention.

It was too late: a flash of burnt yellow shot across my line of vision, and before I knew it, a lioness had leapt out of the bushes and landed right on top of him. Baring her teeth, she sank them deep into the back of his neck.

His little hairy legs kicked like fury, and he yelped and squealed as the big cat turned, vanishing into the bush with her wriggling snack.

"Run!" screamed Mama, flagging up her tail. "Follow me!"

Doing as we were told, we tore after her, absolutely terrified.

I dropped the water pouch and sprinted through the rough, dense undergrowth when, all of a sudden, something sharp grabbed my leg. I pulled and pulled, but my leg wouldn't budge.

"Let go of me!" I ordered, but whatever it was didn't answer. "Ouch! You're hurting me! Let go!" I repeated, but the more I tugged, the tighter it gripped.

When I heard the metallic clunk and a stomach-churning crack, I realised with horror what had happened. I looked down at the rusty poacher's trap as my blood trickled down over the grips.

Luckily, it had been set to catch a much larger animal than myself, so I managed to shove my small tusks between its jagged teeth and prise the spring open. A deep cut exposed a shard of white bone sticking right out of my leg. I retched at the sight of the wound and fought back tears.

I was quite alone and I had to be brave.

I knew I should get home before the hyenas smelled my blood and came after me. As the pain hadn't kicked in yet, I managed to limp along, carrying a leafy branch to brush soil over any telling droplets of blood.

Just then, a rustling sound stopped me in my tracks; something was moving about close by. I held my breath and stood completely still. When I saw it was just the rear end of a 'leopard tortoise' making its slow, plodding way towards the river, I let out a huge sigh of relief.

When I eventually reached home no one was in, not even my grandparents, so I wriggled backwards into the opening to keep an eye out for danger, and as I did so, stabbing pains shot through my leg. Hot tears ran down my cheeks, I panted short, sharp breaths to fight the pain, and then everything went black.

Truffle

Chapter 2

Peter the Ranger to the Rescue

I don't know how long I was unconscious but the next thing I remember was hearing a man's voice and being gently lifted up.

Opening my eyes, I saw it was my friend Peter, the Head Ranger, who looks after the animals on our reserve.

"Poor old you, Happy. It looks like you've been caught in a poacher's trap."

"It was so well hidden, I just didn't see it."

As usual, he was dressed head to toe in khaki-coloured clothes and matching scruffy hat to blend into the scenery. A shabby rucksack hung on one shoulder and a rifle on the other. A cartridge belt hung low on his hips and a sheathed knife poked out from behind it.

He lowered me carefully onto the ground, removed his rucksack and opened a first aid kit.

"Ouch, that's a nasty break, but I think it will heal in a matter of days with my latest remedy. Where was the trap exactly?"

"By the Old Sausage Tree where Solo the lonely elephant sometimes loiters – you know, the big elephant who walks alone?"

"Yes, dear Solo, he is lonely but he shouldn't have been so greedy. His father *had* to teach him a lesson. He'll be let back into the herd once he has learned it. Now you must drink as much of this as you can for pain relief." He placed a bowl of slimy green liquid under my nose. It smelled disgusting but I drank it anyway, and within moments I was feeling rather light-headed.

Next, he filled a syringe full of purple liquid. "This will stop your blood getting infected. You might feel a sharp prick," he added, but because my skin is quite thick I didn't feel a thing.

He cleansed the cut with water before smearing some bright green antiseptic clay on top.

"Now, you *will* feel this," he warned, before counting, "One, two, three," and pushing the broken bone back in place.

"Ouch!" I squealed, my eyes smarting.

Placing some lint on top of the wound, he wrapped a bandage around it, before finally strapping a firm cast around my leg to keep it still.

"So, what happened?"

"A lioness took Truffle and the rest of us just ran for it! It's all my fault; I was supposed to be on lookout."

"Nonsense," replied Peter. "You mustn't blame yourself, lions are very skilled hunters. Anyway, Truffle's a feisty young pig; he just might have got away."

Putting two fingers in his mouth he whistled sharply, and from the shadow of a yellow fever tree came a young, male black rhino. He had beady eyes, and a red-spotted handkerchief neatly tied around his neck.

I couldn't believe my eyes; I'd never met one of these shy animals before, and Mama had always told me that they are very rare animals indeed. In fact, so very rare that black rhinos and white rhinos are close to extinction and need protection before they die out completely. I felt very lucky to meet one.

"This is another youngster I'm looking after. Happiness, this is Little Horn. Little Horn, this is Happiness," introduced Peter.

Looking shyly at me, the calf nodded his heavy head so I nodded back.

Little Horn

Then two dogs came bounding out from the bushes straight towards me and licked my face with slobbery tongues. A very wet welcome!

Peter pulled a net sling out of his rucksack and popped me inside. He carefully slipped my leg through a hole before swinging me onto his back. I liked it; it was really comfortable and I could see for miles.

"I left my truck on Weaver Road," said Peter. "I'm going to take you back to my house until we can find your family."

The dogs led the way with their noses to the ground, zigzagging across the terrain so as not to miss a scent. Little Horn plodded along beside us. I looked down at him and wondered why he wasn't at home with his parents.

Folds of skin were already developing on his shoulders and back like some kind of prehistoric armour plating; he was both ugly and adorable at the same time.

Soon we found the truck, and Peter laid me down in the back. He honked the horn and a large eagle owl with mighty wings and bright orange eyes swooped down silently from a tree and landed on the roof bar. His lethal talons gripped and released the faded, cracked leather in a slow determined motion as he leaned towards me, making strange clucking sounds the whole time.

I shrank back as far as I could, trembling with fear as his sharp beak came closer and closer.

"You can't eat her, Orville; she's one of our guests," said Peter.

"I'm not partial to pig, I'm just having a closer look," said the owl, folding his wings back against his sides. "Sorry to scare you," he added, blinking slowly.

Orville

The dogs leapt into the back with me, curled up and immediately went to sleep. As we started to drive off, a young zebra ran up beside the truck with a small, fluffy mongoose on its back.

"Race you home!" the zebra shouted, galloping off with the mongoose clinging tightly to her mane. 'How bizarre!' I thought to myself, but the smell and warmth of the dogs were comforting, and watching Little Horn's hankie bobbing along behind us made me feel safe. I'd never been on a truck before, and the rocking motion soon sent me to sleep.

Chapter 3

Weaver House Animal Sanctuary

Mango

"Wake up!" said Orville the eagle owl, nudging me gently in the side with his beak. "We're home."

I opened my eyes to see Peter pulling up outside a pair of solid wooden gates. Tall, thorny acacia trees grew either side of them, and a carved wooden sign that read Weaver House Animal Sanctuary hung from their branches. I'd heard all about the sanctuary from Peter but had never actually been inside, so I felt quite excited.

Peter sounded his horn and shouted, "Open up, Mango!"

I heard a key turn and the gates swung open. We drove in and a strange, furry animal in a straw hat (whom I guessed to be Mango) locked the gates behind us.

Peter lifted me out of the sling and handed me to another ranger I know called Harry.

"Harry, find Peggy and ask her to come and check Happiness over, please. Her leg got caught in a poacher's trap. I'm off to destroy it."

"Sure thing. Hey there, Happy!" answered Harry.

Peggy is Peter's wife. She's a vet and tends to the sick animals. Peter and Peggy have one teenage daughter called Hebe who helps them when she's not at school. Harry is a little older than Hebe, he came over from England to help Peggy out last summer and became so attached to an orphaned monkey that he stayed on. He and the monkey are now inseparable, and today it sat on his shoulder busily plaiting a cord.

"I'll go and get Peggy. Don't move, as if you could!" He laughed as he laid me down in the shade of some trees. Above my head, among the branches of the trees, someone had built a house and I wondered who lived there.

While I waited for Harry to return, I watched Little Horn wade into an inviting pond where a pelican was drinking at the water's edge. A colourful chameleon was watching me and without moving a muscle he swivelled one protruding eye and his tongue shot out like a party blower. In an instant, a passing insect was glued to the tip. He sucked it in and swallowed hard.

When Harry returned I asked him, "Who lives in the tree house up there?"

"Ah, that contains the sleeping quarters and nursery for small, sick, or injured animals," he explained. "We care for all sorts here. The patients stay until they are well enough to be released back onto the reserve. The problem is that most of them don't want to leave!"

I shook my head. "I don't mean to be rude, Harry, but I definitely will!"

"We'll see." He gently took the cord from the monkey's paws and tied it around my ankle. "A lucky charm to help you heal quickly," he smiled.

Peggy and Hebe walked across the garden towards me. Hebe was holding hands with Mango (the furry animal who'd opened the gate) who was carrying a basket in his other hand.

"Hey, Happy," said Hebe cheerfully. She knelt down and kissed me on the head. She looked even prettier than the last time I'd seen her. Her lustrous black hair was caught back in a neat ponytail and decorated with beads. She smelled lovely too.

Mango took a bowl out of his basket and filled it with liquid.

"Drink this, please," he ordered. "It's a herbal tincture that will relieve pain and give you calcium to strengthen the bone."

"Thank you," I replied and lapped it up. Meanwhile, Peggy walked up to the pelican in the pond; a small green parrot perched nearby.

"Come here, Flapper," called Peggy to the pelican.

The pelican stopped drinking and took several long, graceful steps towards her.

Peggy very gently extended his wing and pronounced, "Your wing is mended and ready to use; you may leave whenever you want."

"Don't go just yet!" squawked the little green parrot. "I'll miss you so much."

"I'll stay just until the weekend, Flo, and then I really must be off," said Flapper. "I need to see my family again but I'll come back to visit."

Flo dug her small, curved beak into the soft, peachy feathers on her chest and fluffed them up with pleasure.

Peggy left the two birds chatting together and came over to check on me.

"How are you doing, little one? I see you've drunk the medicine." She knelt down and stroked me under the chin.

I started to cry; big, fat teardrops rolled down my face.

"Don't cry, Happy," said Hebe, twiddling the tuft on my tail. "You can't be sad if you are called Happiness!"

"I'm worried about Truffle. Plus, my grandparents are very old and I didn't get them any water," I sniffed. Then I sniffed again for good measure. I was rather enjoying the attention.

"Accidents happen all the time in a wild place like this, you know that, Happiness. Harry and I have helped Mum patch up quite a few recently, haven't we, Harry?" Harry blushed and just beamed at the pretty girl.

"Pass the basket please, Mango. Now, Happiness, eat these berries and then Mango will take you to your bed. You've had a big day and need rest."

I was starving, and I didn't need to be told twice, especially when I saw a large slice of seed cake on top. Delicious.

"Time to take you up to your sleeping quarters," grinned Mango, revealing a large set of chattering teeth. He gathered me up into his unusually long but reassuring arms and carried me up the ramp into the tree house above. He smelled of something unfamiliar but pleasant; a damp and sticky sort of smell.

Upstairs, the wooden floor was covered with clean straw, and the slanted roof – made from a lattice of reeds and rattan – provided good cover from the elements. The canopy of an umbrella tree covered most of the gaps, giving yet further protection. It was really cosy.

Mango laid me down on some soft, fresh hay and wished me a good night's sleep.

I glimpsed a half-moon shining through a small gap in the roof and I whispered to it, "I'm so sorry, Truffle. I love you." I knew my mother would be looking at the moon, too, and thinking of me. "I miss you too, Mama. I'll be home soon."

A few moments later, Hebe came up and sat down beside me with the dogs. "Would you like me to read you a story?" she asked.

"Yes, please." The dogs lay down either side of me.

"I wrote it for my English exam and got an A* for it," Hebe said with pride. "It's about a young girl and an orangutan making hats.

"Once upon a time…" Her soft voice gently faded. I dreamed that I was playing football; my leg didn't hurt at all.

Chapter 4

The Fan Club

Flo

I slept like a log and wondered where I was when I woke up. Someone had pulled back the wicker blinds and sunlight streamed through a large window. When I saw Flo, the parrot, preening her feathers on the branch above me the events of yesterday came flooding back.

"Good morning," I said.

"Morning," she replied through a beak full of down, "Little Horn will be up with your breakfast in a minute."

"Thank you, but I can't stay, I must go home and find out news of my brother."

"You won't be allowed to go home yet, not with that thing on your leg, so you might as well make yourself at home," she chirruped firmly.

Flo was right, Peter would give me news when he had some. I looked around the room; Harry's pet monkey sat in a corner eating peanuts and chucking the empty shells over his shoulder.

I'd never slept so high up before and peering through the window allowed me a bird's-eye view. Everything looked different from above. Small birds darted past, bee-eaters and fly-catchers in search of their breakfast, and far beyond, tea and coffee plantations stretched into the distance. Far, far away the snow-capped top of Mount Kilimanjaro, the tallest mountain in Africa, glistened in the sun. It was a magical sight.

The sound of footsteps made me look towards the ramp. It was Little Horn, the rare rhino, trotting up with a basket of food tied to his neck.

"Breakfast," he announced solemnly.

"Coming!" cried Flo, "I'll help you." She landed on Little

Horn's neck and pecked away at the knot with her small, curved beak until it loosened. Then she held the rope tight, letting the basket down little by little until it touched the ground. Holding her head high, she puffed out her downy chest and a small orange patch of tiny feathers glowed like the African sun.

Little Horn nudged the basket towards me with his wide nose.

"Eat up." His hooked top lip had a piece of shrubbery stuck to it, which had presumably been his breakfast.

"Thank you," I said, chomping away.

Happiness

He watched me eat. "Finish it all up. You need to get better." His shiny black eyes were as innocent as a baby's and full of sadness.

"Excuse me asking, but why do you wear handkerchiefs around your neck?"

"They're lucky charms, to stop poachers killing me," he replied simply, before adding, "They won't try yet, but they will when my horns grow." Close up, I could see that although Little Horn's skin was thick, it wasn't thick enough to stop a bullet if a poacher wanted to kill him.

"I've got one too," I said. "On my ankle." I raised my good leg in the air.

"You have to believe in it, you know, otherwise, it won't work," replied Little Horn. "Just close your eyes and believe. And make a wish too, if you like."

I closed my eyes tight and made two wishes. I wished that baby animals would never ever need to wear a lucky charm to stop them being killed and I wished the poachers would go away forever.

I opened my eyes. "Harry gave me my lucky charm, where did you get yours from?"

"My fan club. Harry writes a blog and tweets about the animals that live here and thousands of people all over the world donate money towards the upkeep of our home or they adopt us. I've got lots of parents who send me hankies because they want to save the rhinos before it's too late."

"I'm so happy to meet you. You're the first one I've ever met," I admitted.

Little Horn lay down in the shade and sighed. Our chat was interrupted by the sound of the zebra trotting up the ramp. The mongoose still clung firmly to her back! Peter and Mango followed behind, pushing a wheelbarrow full of hay and a basket of fruit.

"Fresh bedding," Mango chattered.

"I hope you slept well," said Peter, heaving bales of clean hay out from the barrow. He swiftly made up clean beds and carefully moved me onto one of them.

Orville, the eagle owl, swept silently down from his home in the ebony tree and perched on the window frame. "How's the patient?" he squawked.

"A bit better, thank you, and I've had breakfast in bed for the first time in my life!"

"Peter, I've been telling Happiness all about Harry's blog and the adoptions and my lucky hankies," said Little Horn.

"Excellent," said Peter. He plonked himself down on a tree stump, pulled the basket close to him and took out an orange. He spoke slowly as he carefully removed the peel. "Harry started writing it last year to keep people informed of our work out here. We're mainly a charity so we need a constant flow of money to survive. With their donations, and the profits from our home-grown produce, we're just about keeping afloat – but we need more funds to buy tracking collars for some of the animals."

"Why don't you just catch the poachers?" I asked naively.

"Sometimes we do, but it's getting harder. They're very professional and organised, and nowadays they use speedboats and helicopters to get away."

I thought about this for a moment. "Why don't you tell the ones you catch to stop?"

Peter let out a deep sigh. "Unfortunately, they're too well

paid by the people who hire them, so they don't want to. But a new law means that anyone involved in illegal wildlife trade can either be given a hefty fine or go to jail for seven years. During their stretch, I want to open workshops in the jail and teach them the error of their ways, and perhaps even offer them jobs as rangers after their release."

"Some local people kill elephants too, don't they?" I asked.

Peter nodded. "Yes, when they get too close to their villages and trample their crops. I need funds to erect strong fencing to keep the animals and the people apart. Some of the villagers work for me now, and I want them to attend a college to train them on how to manage the wildlife."

"You could call it *A College for Poachers Turned Gamekeepers*," I suggested.

"S-T-R-E-T-C-H! He needs an injection of C-A-S-H!" said Mango, pronouncing the letters one by one.

"I haven't got any money," I admitted. "But I'll help you catch the men before I leave here."

Smiling down at me, Peter patted my head. I could tell he didn't believe me.

Chapter 5

The Star Attraction

The zebra stood quietly in the shade and a shaft of sunlight coming through the roof caught a jagged scar on her side.

"How did she get that scar?" I asked Peter quietly.

"Zizi?" Peter asked, looking across at the zebra. "A lion nearly killed her. She's a beauty, isn't she? Did you know that every single zebra has different markings, much like people's fingerprints?" He turned his hand over and showed me his. Each finger pad was etched in curious swirling patterns and was much harder to see than Zizi's stripes.

Zizi trotted over to join us. "I heard you talking about me. If you really want to know, a lioness ambushed my herd," she said. "We scattered in different directions to confuse her but I wasn't fast enough; she jumped on my back, dug her claws into my side and dragged me down. I kicked really hard until she released her grip but her claws had torn open my side. I lost a lot of blood but luckily Peter found me the same day, and Peggy and Hebe stitched me up just like new."

"My turn! Can I tell my story please?" asked the mongoose, jumping up and down excitedly.

"Calm down, Monty," ordered Orville sharply. "And stop fidgeting!" The little mongoose sat up on his hind legs and spread out his bushy tail for balance. As he spoke in an overly dramatic, squeaky voice, his little pink nose moved up and down like a rabbit's.

"I was stealing eggs from a bird's nest when I felt the coils of a giant rock python tightening around my middle," he began, obviously enjoying the attention. "I sank my teeth into the snake's head until it released its grip. With great agility and some adept twists and turns, I wriggled free and sprinted for miles until I collapsed outside the gates here. Peggy found me hiding under a bush, exhausted, hungry and scared." He looked around at us all, clearly hoping for sympathy, but as no one said anything, he carried on.

"She took me in, listened to my tale of woe and, appreciating how incredibly brave I'd been, told me that if I promised not to steal any more I could stay. Of course, I promised."

"A giant python indeed," muttered Orville behind his wing.

"It's true! Anyway, what are you doing hanging around here? You should be catching mice!" he piped cheekily.

"You know perfectly well that I work here, Monty," tutted Orville. "Without me, the place would be, umm, well, less safe."

"He's our night spotter," Peter explained.

"What's that?" I asked curiously.

"He flies around at night to spot the poachers' movements and tell us of any sightings. He's very useful as he can see for miles. The problem is, by the time we get there, they've usually moved on. It's as if they know we are coming," he said, looking puzzled.

"Did you spot Truffle last night, Orville?" I asked.

"No sign yet but don't lose heart," he said kindly.

During the storytelling, Mango had been practising forward somersaults across the floor and gathering bits of straw on his fur as he rolled.

"Excuse me, Peter. But what exactly is Mango?" I whispered.

"I suppose you've never seen a Mango before?"

"Never," I confirmed, shaking my head. "I have seen lots of monkeys, but none with such very long arms!"

The russet-coloured ball of fur rolled over to me, stopping a fraction away from my broken leg. He stood up and stretched. "I'm the only orangutan in East Africa," he said, proudly pounding his hairy chest.

"Where do you come from?" I asked.

Plunging his hand into the fruit basket, he rummaged around until he pulled out the largest banana he could find, peeled it lovingly and chucked the skin over his shoulder.

Mango

"I lived with my mother and sister in a gi-nor-mous, lush, tropical forest, far away from here. Borneo, In-do-ne-sia." He pronounced the words carefully as he waved his free arm around in the air until it located a branch to hang on to.

Swaying gently from side to side he finished the banana and then picked up on his story. "We built our nests in the canopy at the top of the trees where we spent all our time, as it supplied everything we needed. The leaves collected rainwater and the foliage supplied flowers, berries, crunchy insects and dozens of mushy fruits to eat."

He curled his feet firmly around the branch, leaving his hands free to rummage in the fruit basket. "This is my favourite!" he said suddenly, taking such a large bite out of a plump mango that his cheeks bulged and the juices ran over his face. "When we weren't eating we would play games, groom each other, or sleep. Sheer bliss," he slurped and closed his eyes dreamily.

"What happened?" I said, almost too afraid to ask.

"It was destroyed by *lum-ber-jacks*!" he spluttered. "*De-for-es-ta-tion*!" He released the branch and landed silently on his soft padded feet.

"Men drove up in lorries and used noisy chainsaws to cut down our homes. *'TIMBER!'* they bellowed, as each magnificent tree crashed to the ground. Young men rode forlorn elephants, kicking them repeatedly behind the ears to make them work harder. The exhausted creatures heaved vast tree trunks around from dawn until dusk, and the men hit them with sticks if they tried to rest. Most of the forest animals and birds fled but we stayed as long as we could, hoping the men wouldn't come back."

"Then what happened?" I asked. The hairs on the back of my neck bristled with anticipation.

"They *did* come back and we tried to run away but it was too late. They caught us easily in nets, bundled me into one crate and my mother and sister into another, and one of them drove me for hours across hot, bumpy terrain without any food or water. I rattled the bars until my hands bled but the driver only shouted at me to sit still. I felt so carsick and was thankful when we finally stopped moving. I watched as money was exchanged between the cruel driver and a *mean*-looking man in a uniform."

Mango paused and stared into the distance. He shook his head as if to rid his mind of the awful memories.

"'Thanks, mate,' said the mean man. 'This ugly beast is going to make me rich!'

"I didn't understand at first," Mango went on, "but when I saw dozens of caged animals and birds, I knew it had to be some kind of circus. Only the insects ran free."

'Like the little five,' I thought solemnly. "Were you scared?" I whispered, trembling all over.

"Terrified," he nodded. "Everything was new and strange to me, and I felt completely alone. I heard lions and tigers growling, and I watched the elephants pace up and down with their heads bowed and a distant look in their eyes."

Mango paused for a moment to reflect, and tears welled up in his eyes. "It was the first time I've ever been afraid of the dark. I'd never been on my own before or slept on a floor, and my bed smelled strange and the animals cried out all night. I couldn't sleep a wink.

"Mind you, I had a keeper who was quite kind. He kept my cage clean and every day he would teach me new skills: magic tricks, how to draw, play catch and make paper hats. Hundreds of hats in assorted colours and shapes. I had to make six an hour but I found them easy and he gave me treats when I met my daily target.

"But sometimes Mr Mean came too and he made me learn the hardest thing of all."

"What was that?"

"To fly a helicopter!"

"A real helicopter, that's awesome!"

"No, not a real one! He stuck me in front of a simulator screen which had lots of complicated dials and a gear stick. I had to fly it over a make-believe game reserve capturing innocent animals in a net, reel them in and drop them in a cage."

"What a horrid game! And it must have been so hard to do."

"It was impossible at first but that man had such a cruel streak in him and actually enjoyed watching me suffer! When I first tried and failed over and over again, he would poke me with a sharp stick and taunt me, saying that I would never see my family again and then he would laugh and laugh. But I refused to cry in front of him and I remembered my mother once telling me that we are almost as clever as humans so I was determined to do it.

"It took weeks of practice but now I think I could actually fly a real one. In a real emergency, that is."

"Wow, that's amazing. Let's hope there's a real emergency and you can take me with you! Nothing too serious, though, just a mini-emergency. Do go on."

"I was advertised in the local newspaper as 'The Star Attraction' along with a photograph of my keeper playing with me in order to attract visitors. I know because he pinned one up in my cage and said I should be proud of how far I had come.

"Then one evening Mr Mean turned up with a big, fat smile on his face. He dressed me in an old pilot's hat, goggles and leather jacket. Then he put a rope around my ankle, walked me into the circus ring and tied me to a peg in the ground. He said I was ready to 'entertain the crowd' and that I would be called *The Ginger Controller* from now on because I have red fur.

"Different families came every afternoon and evening. They slurped their drinks through plastic straws, rustled crisp packets and munched on sweets. After the poor elephants and tigers had been made to perform their acts, the audience would chant repeatedly for their favourite performance. 'We want Ginger! We want Ginger!'

"In the interval, before I went on, my keeper went around selling my paper hats to the crowd but I never got a penny for them.

"Everyone watched me on a huge projector and shouted and cheered if I caught something, or whistled and booed if I didn't. If I crashed, the audience laughed and threw bananas at me. The more they laughed, the more humiliated I felt, until one night I threw a mug at Mr Mean and it struck him square on the jaw. The crowd applauded but he smacked me really hard so I punched him back and knocked him out. My keeper tried not to laugh and he was told to take me back to my cage and leave me there for days without food or water as punishment."

Peter took in a deep breath. "I heard about Mango on the news. Luckily, somebody complained about Mango's treatment and the circus was investigated, fined, and closed down. The animals were put up for sale and I bought him. They said he was a *dangerous animal* and were happy to be rid of him!" Mango pouted and kissed Peter lovingly on his forehead.

"Where are your mother and sister now?" I asked.

"Peter found out they're living in a lovely conservation park in Borneo. They have huge, open spaces to roam free, and they're safe from loggers, but they miss me terribly, so he's arranging for them to come and live here!" Mango helped himself to a handful of peanuts.

"I think your eyes are bigger than your stomach, Mango!" said Peter, moving the basket away.

"A growing monkey *needs* to eat a lot! I love it here – Peggy's teaching me to cook and I'm learning to make real hats with Hebe," he said, crunching cheerfully on his snack.

"An orangutan making hats!" hooted Orville. "Whatever next?"

"You'll see. If I can make paper hats, I can make real ones!" Mango said, indignantly. He snatched up a bunch of grapes and started to sort through a pile of leaves.

Chapter 6

Big Horn

Little Horn

"Peter?" asked Monty, noisily sucking on a hen's egg.

"Yes, Monty?"

"Why *do* they chop the trees down?"

"The indigenous ones have no real value to people, but the palm oil trees they plant in their place are fast growing and can be sold after a few years," he explained.

"What does 'indigenous' mean?"

"Something that grows there naturally. Palm oil is used in cooking, food, cosmetics, washing powder and even in some animal feed, so there's loads of money to be made," continued Peter.

"Like poachers make money?"

"Exactly, Monty. Unfortunately, it leaves hundreds of animals homeless, and, without food or shelter, they die. Not to mention the devastation to the rainforests."

Monty thought about this for a moment, scratched his head with his tiny paw and asked, "Why do people buy rhino horn and elephant tusks?"

"Some countries believe that rhino horn has medicinal properties. Others want jewellery or ornaments made from ivory, or they keep a whole elephant tusk as a souvenir."

"Is that why Little Horn is here, because of poachers?"

"Yes, I'm afraid it is, Monty," Peter said, bowing his head.

Just then, Little Horn got to his feet, his small tail curled in tightly between his hind legs.

"I'll tell you why. My family and I were minding our own business munching grass when we heard a strange rustling sound. It was dusk, and as our eyesight is poor and there was no wind, we couldn't see or smell anyone. Before we knew it, two poachers crept out from the trees and shot my father, Big Horn, at close range! He dropped down dead and everyone ran for cover except me. I was too scared to move; I just didn't know what to do. They didn't see me but I saw them take my father's horn and drive away." Tears rolled down his dusty cheeks as he remembered that horrific day.

"There, there," reassured Orville. "Old Biggie Big Horn wouldn't have known anything about it: it was all over too quickly for him to suffer."

"But I'm suffering. I miss him so much," he sobbed.

Peter put his arms around Little Horn. "I know, dear boy, it's terrible. I promise that I'll reunite you with your mother, but only when it's safe and not a minute before. Flo told her that you are safe here with us and she's waiting until she can come and get you."

"I'm so lucky you saved me. I love you, Peter."

"I love you too." Peter gently dabbed Little Horn's tears.

"Where do you come from, Happy?" Little Horn sniffed, quickly changing the subject.

"I live in a den under an ebony tree with my mother, my grandparents, my brothers, Truffle and Quiver, and my sister, Winkle."

"Silly names," muttered Monty under his breath. The owl gave him a very hard stare. "Why do your grandparents live with you?" asked Monty, looking embarrassed and quickly washing behind his ears.

"Because they are elderly and they need taking care of," I

explained. "I run errands for them – like fetching food and water – and they give me lessons in return."

"What kind of lessons?" asked Monty curiously.

"Every Sunday at dawn they open their school under the Wait-A-Bit Acacia Tree, and anyone can join in. Sometimes they take us on walks and teach us the names of trees and shrubs, how to track spoors, the difference between poisonous or medicinal plants, and how to identify droppings and footprints, that kind of thing. Elephants are the easiest for identification, as their feet are very large and their heaps of dung are the size of termite hills."

"Why do you need to know all this?" Monty giggled, visualising big piles of dung.

"If I see fresh prints left by a lion or poacher, I can run away quickly, or if I want to find a friend, I can follow their tracks," I explained.

"Or poo?" sniggered Monty.

I ignored him and carried on. "The names of the planets and clouds… when to expect a full moon… and when the short or long rains will come. The local tribes come and tell us stories too."

"Which tribes?" asked Monty sitting up tall. "I've only ever met the Masai."

"Them and the Chagga, Kikuyu, Wakamba. They are gentle people and they don't eat warthogs!"

"You must be very clever, learning all these things," he said, sounding impressed.

"Not really; Grandpa says I have a thirst for knowledge."

Chapter 7

The Kitchen Garden

Harry rumbled up the ramp pushing a wooden cart. "Morning all," he said, cheerfully. "Who would like to show Happiness around the grounds?"

"Me, me, me!" shouted Monty, jumping up. He'd had enough of sitting still.

"I will," said Mango. "This hat is just not working out as it's meant to."

The orangutan was covered from head to foot in moss, twigs and leaves. Slapping a sticky, gooey mess on his head, he peered into a cracked mirror propped against a tree and then back at the magazine he was holding in his hand.

"It's not quite like the picture," he said, turning around and straining to see the view from the back.

"It's coming along," said Peter politely, as he helped pull bits of moss off Mango's ears. "But perhaps use less glue next time?" It was then that I realised his funny sticky smell must be that stuff called glue.

Mango shrugged. "Hebe and I are working on a new hat design using, and I quote, 'organic, generic, indigenous, locally available sustainable materials and resources, thus making a sustainable source of supply', or something along those lines."

"What does that mean?" I asked, more than a little confused.

"I'm not sure exactly," admitted Mango. "I read it here," he said, poking the page that was now firmly glued to his hand. "I think it means that if I use what I have around me, don't use it all up at once and let it have time to grow again then I won't run out of supplies or damage nature."

"So, if lumberjacks stopped chopping the trees down and

poachers stopped shooting rhinos and elephants, there would be enough of them too?" I asked.

"Precisely," said Mango, pulling the gummy mess off his head and carefully placing it on the ground to dry. He popped his familiar straw hat back on and tugged the magazine off his hand. Harry handed him some keys, an apron and a pair of secateurs.

Mango slung the keys around his neck, tied the apron around his rotund middle and dropped the secateurs into a pocket. Then he grabbed a handful of peanuts. "Just in case I get peckish."

Harry settled me into the cart next to a spade and some bird food and wheeled me down the ramp followed excitedly by the others. Then he secured two baskets across Zizi's back.

"Listen, Mango, we need ripe fruits, cocoa pods, eggs, honey, tomatoes, lettuce and potatoes, please. Have a good day, everyone."

Mango smacked his lips in anticipation.

"And don't forget to feed the hens. Peter and I will be out all day on the reserve looking for your family, Happiness."

"Off we go, no time to waste!" commanded Mango. He pushed me beneath an avenue of cocoa trees. Their ripe green-and-yellow pods dangled down, ready to drop at any moment.

Reaching up, he snipped a dozen and laid them lovingly in the baskets.

"I'll use them for ice cream this week, but normally we make cocoa powder from the pods and sell it to a company that makes chocolate bars," he explained, licking his lips. "The *chocolatey* firm always send me a box on my birthday!"

"When's your birthday, Mango?" I asked.

"I'm not certain. Soon, I think," he replied. "I'll have to ask Peggy. It'll be my third birthday."

"I've never had a birthday," said Little Horn thoughtfully.

"Then you can have your first birthday with me; we'll all have one together," offered Mango.

"I've had one, so I'll be two," I remembered.

Carrying on, we trundled through a gateway into an orchard bursting with fruit trees.

"We grow pineapples, cherries, oranges, mangoes, pawpaws and peaches," Mango explained, carefully selecting an assortment of ripe fruits and putting them in the baskets.

"I can carry more," offered Zizi. "It's not very heavy yet. I know! Let's take Happy to the Kitchen Garden." She nudged open a small wooden gate with her head.

"Vegetables galore," piped up Monty, scampering ahead. He ran from plant to plant sniffing and nibbling each one in turn.

"We grow beans, potatoes, carrots and kale in this row. Tomatoes, lettuces, spinach and pigweed are in the second row," he announced proudly.

"And strawberries!" said Mango, popping the largest one in his mouth. Once he had finished with his strawberry, he picked a large bunch of pigweed – my favourite snack – and handed it to me. I snaffled it down while he dug up a big pile of earthy new potatoes. Then he pulled up some lettuces and snipped off several bunches of ripe, red tomatoes.

I spotted Monty disappearing through an archway.

"Where's he going now?" I asked.

"To the Physic Garden. Let's follow him."

Once we'd caught up, Monty was desperate to tell me all about the garden. "This is where Peter grows plants to make medicines, herbs for tea and stinging nettles for soup. And con-coc-tions, which turn into things called *anti-sep-tic* and *anaes-the-tic.*"

"What's in the house over there?" I asked, glancing over at a small glass building.

"Aha! We're not allowed in the greenhouse. It's full of deadly, poisonous plants to kill deadly snakes and scorpions. Come and see what else we have, though." With that, Monty squeezed himself under a gate and scurried ahead.

"I know where he's gone!" said Mango, trundling after him, and we soon found him standing among some hens, sucking one of their eggs.

Mango scattered the bird food on the ground and, in turn, the hens stood up and let him collect their warm, freshly laid eggs.

Next to the hen-house was a beehive, and an extremely large bee squeezed herself out from the hive's entrance with a pop and landed woozily on a table next to a bowl of honey. She had a small crown of pollen around her head.

"Help yourselves to anything you need. We've made plenty to go round," she offered generously.

"Little hoglet, you must be the new patient I've heard about. I hope you'll be very happy here," she buzzed. "Help yourself to my honey. It's good for you. Wipe some on your wound too, it's got healing powers."

"Thank you but I'm not staying, I'm only here until my leg gets better, and then I'll be off home."

"We'll see," she said knowingly.

Mango took the bowl of honey and thanked her very much.

"Come on, let's show Happiness the plantations now," suggested Little Horn, running off happily. He had perked up considerably since breakfast.

"There's more, Little Horn?" I asked.

He nodded hard.

We followed him down a long path until we reached a wire fence. Stretching out below us and as far as the eye could see, were rows and rows of tea and coffee bushes.

There were several workers dispersed between the rows, and when they saw me they waved. I recognised them because they had brought tea-leaves and coffee beans into school one morning.

"Peter sells them to help pay for our expenses, and to buy food for the farm animals," explained Little Horn.

"There are farm animals as well?"

"Oh yes, the sanctuary is *almost* totally self-sufficient," said Mango, before adding anxiously, "I think we'd better get back now; it's nearly supper time." It was clear he didn't want to miss it.

When we got back, Peter and Harry were also home from their day out on the reserve.

"We've got incredible news for you, Happiness," said Peter grinning from ear to ear. "Truffle's home, safe and well!"

"He's still alive and wasn't eaten?" I gasped. I could hardly believe it.

"Yes, alive and kicking! It just so happens that the lioness that took him was going to share Truffle with her husband, who is my friend Zulu. Zulu had heard that I was looking after you and when he realised Truffle was your brother they let him go. You see, last year when he was injured by a poacher's stray bullet, I dug it out and saved his life, so now he's done us a favour in return."

I could hardly believe my ears. "So can I go home now?"

"Absolutely not; it's not safe," said Harry. "Orville spotted two men creeping around near the clearing, and they took off in a helicopter. I expect they're after elephants, so they'll be back. They usually scout around to check where the herd is and come back when there's a full moon and cloudless sky for good vision."

"That's when my birthday is: when there's a full moon!" chattered Mango excitedly.

Harry frowned. "That can't be right, Mango. There are thirteen full moons in a year, and you can only have one birthday every year."

"Well, it's on one of them. My mother would always tell me which one so I don't actually know."

"It doesn't matter. You can have it on the next full moon but only if the poachers have been caught first."

As I was listening to the conversation, I tried to scratch my leg.

"Here, let me," said Harry, lifting me out of the cart. He

shoved a stick down inside the plaster and wiggled it about.

"I have a better idea," suggested Peter, "let's take it off. The bone should be set by now. Have a swim: the salts are healing. And then you can eat your supper." With that, he gently removed the cast. "You're healing well. I'll put some fresh bandages on after your swim."

"The queen bee told me to put honey on it too!"

"Race you in!" challenged Little Horn, dashing off towards the water.

I hobbled after him and slid in on my tummy; the water was cool and soothing. It wasn't very deep so we just went in until our backs were covered and paddled about.

Mango sat down at the water's edge and drew patterns in the earth with his stick.

"I'm going to catch the poachers so you can go home to your mother," I whispered to Little Horn.

"How?" he said, staring at me intently.

"I'll put my thinking cap on and come up with a plan," I assured him.

"I've never seen a thinking cap," said Mango looking up from his drawing. "What do they look like?"

"It's just a figure of speech," I giggled, rolling onto my back.

Part II

Happiness Hatches Her Plans

Farm Animals

Back in my cosy bed that night, I made a promise to myself that I, Happiness Hazel Horner, would help catch the killers so that no baby animal ever had to wear a lucky charm again. No matter what it took.

I tossed and turned until daylight, trying to formulate a plan in my mind, and before I knew it, Peggy was ringing the breakfast gong.

The noise woke Little Horn who had been in a deep sleep. "Let's go and see the farm animals," he suggested blearily, "but we have to get permission from Peter first."

"But not before breakfast," said Mango, swinging down from his nest above our heads.

We met up with Zizi and Monty downstairs and after a

hearty breakfast made our way over to Weaver House with Little Horn leading the way. It was built on stilts like our tree house and its thatched roof almost touched the ground. A chimney poked out of the top and the windows were screened with woven blinds to keep the mosquitoes out. We made our way up the ramp, across the veranda and into the sitting room.

"I'm going to the kitchen. See you later," said Mango, bustling off.

A ceiling fan circled gently round and round creating a gentle breeze, and hand-tied bunches of herbs, roses and seed-pods hung upside down from the roof rafters to dry. A canvas hammock swayed in one corner, and, on hearing our approach, a small head with eyes half closed peered sleepily over the top.

"Hey, Ben!" said Monty.

"Hey," said a tiny, shaky voice. "I'm still sleeping." With that, the little bushbaby fell silent.

Peter and Harry were sitting side by side at a large desk in the corner staring at a computer.

"Good morning, I see you are walking quite well, Happy," observed Peter.

"Yes, thanks. It feels much better already."

"Aha," said Harry, "just who I need! I've got to take your photo and add it to the website. Stand still in the sunlight, will you?"

I did as I was asked and he took lots of photos from different angles. After checking the shots, he nodded to himself. "Perfect, I'll soon have you adopted!"

"But can I still go home if I get adopted?" I asked, slightly alarmed.

"Of course!"

Relieved, I glanced around the room. It was simply furnished but the walls were plastered with photographs of African wildlife; each and every one was named and numbered, including my new friends. Harry talked me through every photograph, explaining who the animal was and how they had been helped or protected. They had helped hundreds and hundreds of animals so I could see why they needed money.

Hebe was sitting on a wooden stool, stitching ribbon onto a hat. "Come here, Happiness," she called, and when I trotted over she placed the hat on my head. "Your ears are too big!" She laughed and kissed me on the snout.

I liked Hebe; she smelled of coconuts and violet flowers all wrapped into one. And she was so pretty. I noticed Harry admiring her secretly from the corner of his eye.

"One day, Mango and I are going to sell enough hats to buy tracking collars for the elephants and rhinos as well as drones to follow their movements."

"That'll take a lot of hats," teased Harry, "and don't forget we need infra-red cameras too!" Hebe blushed coyly.

Mango popped his head round the kitchen door. "I'm making ice cream!" he shouted at the top of his voice. We could see that because he had rather a lot of it smeared around his mouth and a lot more stuck to his fur.

"It's a new *re-ci-pe* of mine," he declared, waving a wooden spoon around in the air. "I'm experimenting with marshmallows, strawberries and cocoa powder. It will be delectable!"

"Well, when you've finished, come and help me with this hat," said Hebe fondly.

Little Horn nudged Peter in the thigh. "Please, Peter, may we see the farm animals?"

Peter stood up. "Of course, young man."

"Follow me," shouted Monty, dashing ahead.

As we passed the kitchen, Peter stopped dead in his tracks.

"Oh dear, you'd better clean up before Peggy sees this mess!" Dirty pots and pans covered every surface. Mixing bowls and whisks dripped a sticky pink and brown substance onto the floor. Mango wiped the spoon across his tummy and dipped it into a large bowl.

"Peggy wasn't here so I thought I'd surprise her. A taster, anyone?"

"Not just yet, Mango. Maybe later," said Peter tactfully. We made our way down another ramp to a backyard with a field beyond. In the field, there were four goats, numerous cows and a huge white bull.

"You have everything, like Mango's forest!" I said.

"Yes," said Peter. "The goats and cows provide us with milk and cheese; the bull helps us with heavy workloads."

"Quick, come and see the pigs," shrilled Monty, "she's had babies!"

"Pigs, as well," I said, trotting over to the pigsty.

"One, two, three, four, five, six, seven, eight!" counted Monty. "She's had eight piglets in the night!"

The tired mother was lying on her side. Her newborns clambered over each other to drink while the proud father chomped down on some potato peelings.

"What do they provide?" I asked, staring at the tiny pink animals.

"The adults find truffles to make truffle oil, another product we sell," explained Peter.

"Crikey, who on earth are they?" squeaked Monty. Two spikey creatures with pointy things in their mouths, scuttled past us.

Peter bent down. "Hello there. May I help you?"

"Oooh, h– h– hello," stuttered one. "I wondered if we could st– st– st– stay for a while? We've just got married and need a home. My name is Spike, and this is my w– w– w– wife, Holly," he said shyly, looking at his blushing bride.

"Congratulations!" said Peter to the newly wed porcupines. "And you are very welcome. Would you like a hand with those?"

"Yes, p– p– p– please," said Spike. "I'm trying to stack some old quills in a neat p– p– p– pile: they're useful for games," he explained, arranging a bundle of quills with his nose.

"Let me help you," said Peter, gathering them up. "You can make a home under my house."

"Two more mouths to feed!" I said, looking up at Peter.

"Everyone's welcome!" he grinned.

Spike and Holly

Chapter 9

The Football Match

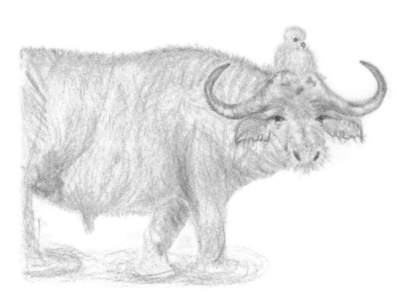

Buffy and Flo

My name is Happiness

"Come along, everyone, it's time for Happy to meet Buffy," said Peter. "He's waiting at the gates and has offered to take you all out for some exercise. In the old days, he was quite dangerous, but he's mellowed over the years, so you're in safe hands." Peter smiled reassuringly.

We walked around the house to the gates I had first come through when rescued.

"Morning, young lady. Nice to meet you," said the old buffalo gruffly. He squinted down at me and I felt the warm air from his wide nostrils tickle my face.

His curled horns were caked in mud and his battle-torn ears twitched constantly. Ben the bushbaby had obviously woken up because he was sitting between them, helping to shoo flies away while Flo the pretty parrot perched on his broad back, gently pecking off any small insects that she fancied. Monty ran up one of his legs and settled down to wash. Zizi kicked at the dry earth with her hooves, impatient to get going.

"I'm a bit arthritic, so I can't walk very fast." Buffy lumbered off, humming to himself.

"I'm scared. I want to go home," whispered Little Horn.

"Stick with me. I'll look after you," I reassured him.

"Everyone here, present and correct?" asked Monty from above.

"Wait for me," called Mango running over. He had a whistle and a bag of cards hung around his neck, and he clutched a football and a bunch of bananas tightly to his chest. Traces of ice cream were still stuck to his fur. Our procession set off slowly down the path towards the riverbank.

67

"Do you know about the little five?" I asked Little Horn.

"Never heard of them. Am I one of them?"

"No, you're one of the Big Five! I'll point them out to you as we go."

After a while, the army ants came marching towards us, out on their daily morning exercise. Army ants have a very strict regime of exercise.

"Left, right, left, right. Halt!" ordered the General, raising one leg in the air. The small ants that had been marching down the centre of the line immediately sat down on the parched earth, but the bigger soldier ants that flanked them stood stiffly to attention.

"Morning, General," said the buffalo.

The minuscule leader turned proudly from his troops. "Morning, Buffy! Where are you going?"

"Taking the youngsters out for the day; exercise is good for them," he explained in a fatherly manner.

The General nodded. "Mind how you go; I noticed some fresh human tracks down by the river." He glanced at his troops again. "Better not hang around; we're building some new barracks. Attention! On your feet, everyone! Quick march!" he barked.

The tired ants dusted themselves down and continued on their way.

After a while, we came to the exact spot by the Sausage Tree where I'd been caught in the trap. Thankfully, the trap had been removed, as Peter had promised. Solo, the lonely elephant, was loitering around, looking particularly outcast today.

Solo

"Any news from your father, Solo?" grunted Buffy to the elephant.

"Nothing," replied the despondent creature in a deep baritone voice.

"Can't you think of *something* to please him?" asked Buffy.

Solo shook his head from side to side. "Hello, Happiness," he said when he noticed me. "Good news about your bro!" Dragging his limp trunk, he strolled off into the trees and we continued on our journey.

"Why isn't he with his herd?" asked Little Horn.

"His mother sent him on an errand to fetch some bananas, but he came home without any, saying he just couldn't help himself – he'd eaten the lot. His father, Eddie, said that he must do one good deed to be allowed back into the herd," explained Buffy.

'Hmm,' I thought to myself. 'If he helps me catch the poachers then that would be a very good deed indeed.'

When we finally reached the river, Buffy paused at the bank. "Hey, chaps!" he called across to his family grazing on the far side. They didn't answer him. "Miserable bunch – they're just no fun; all they do is eat or fight. No sense of humour, either; that's why I don't mix with them any more and, what's worse, they don't even seem to care." He stared at them, looking a little sad, or a little annoyed; I couldn't quite tell which.

"But we love you. You're such fun to be with!" reassured Monty.

"Am I really?" he said, clearly tickled pink by the compliment.

"You bet!" squeaked Ben.

Mr and Mrs Twiga – the tallest giraffes on the reserve – were standing further down the bank, stamping their feet and staring hard into the distance, completely unaware of our presence. I wondered what they were looking for.

Buffy noticed the fresh shoe prints that went down to the water's edge. "These are definitely not Harry's or Peter's shoes," he said ominously.

"I thought we came out for some exercise," said Mango, blowing his whistle. "What shall we play today, Buffy? Football with the young hippos?"

Monty and Ben glanced over at each other, shaking their heads.

"Hippos are scary," they said in unison.

"I don't mean to be rude, but I think they're very dangerous too," I added, my voice trailing off shyly.

"They'll behave with me around, I promise, so don't you worry!" Buffy assured us.

The hippo parents floated about on the surface of the water, watching us closely. They had a habit of disappearing underwater for minutes at a time and re-surfacing just where you didn't expect them. It was most disconcerting. Their children, however, were playing further downstream, so we went along to join them.

"We've been seeing who can hold their breath the longest," said one of the hippos, bobbing up suddenly.

"Hello, Gussy," called Little Horn. "Meet Happiness, our new best friend."

Gussy

Six small, round calves emerged from the water and greeted me with a variety of gurgling sounds.

"Where's your brother, Hugo?" asked Buffy.

"He was playing with us a minute ago," said the smallest one, who was having fun blowing bubbles. "He'll turn up. He always does."

Just then, Harry drew up in a speedboat.

"We're going to play football," said Mango. "Want to play?"

"Another time," replied Harry. "There's been a sighting of a poacher's boat upstream." With that, he revved up the engine and sped off along the water, weaving skilfully between the hippos.

"Can we referee?" chorused Ben and Monty.

Mango took the whistle and cards from his pouch and handed the whistle to Ben and the cards to Monty. Lastly, he arranged some branches into goalposts at each end of a clearing and then turned to the others. "Divide yourselves up into teams. We really could do with more players," he said, scratching his armpit. "But we'll just have to manage somehow. You mind your leg, Happy, and just do what you can."

"Rough or smooth?" he asked, flipping a dry dung pat into the air.

"Smooth," I replied.

"Smooth it is, so you kick off. We'll both be captains." Mango looked at the others. "To make it fair, Little Horn can play on your team and Zizi on mine – with three hippos per side. Ready? On the count of three. One, two–!"

'Three' was accompanied by the sound of running feet,

and my family bursting through the bushes completely unannounced.

"Happiness!" they squealed in unison.

We circled round and round each other, snuffling and pressing our snouts together in greeting until I felt quite dizzy.

"Solo told us you were living at Weaver House," said Papa.

"Is your leg broken?" asked Quiver and shivered.

Quiver

"Look at my neck," Truffle said, showing me his scar.

"Zulu let you go!" I said.

"Not before I kicked his wicked wife's tooth out!" he snorted proudly.

"Why's the rhino wearing a hankie?" tittered Winkle, staring at Little Horn.

"I'll explain later, little Winkle," I promised, nestling in close to her. I've always felt very protective of my sister because she's particularly small.

"Dearest Happiness, we looked everywhere for you," Mama said, pressing her snout hard against mine and fighting back tears. She had unfamiliar white whiskers all over her chin, and there were some new worry wrinkles around her eyes.

"Oh, Mama, I'm so sorry I worried you. I missed you all so much. I looked at the moon each night like you told me to do if we ever got separated."

"So did we, darling, every single night." Mama smiled. Her wrinkles suddenly looked like laughter lines and, although she had definitely aged a bit, she was still beautiful.

Papa gave me a loving scratch with his tusks and grunted softly. I noticed he had some new facial warts that made him look even more handsome.

Then, my beloved grandparents – who had been standing patiently by – muscled in and took their turns to kiss me.

"How are you, dearest? We've been so worried," Grandma said, her voice trembling with emotion. She had clearly aged, too, but I didn't say anything. I suppose it was all the fright about Truffle being nearly killed and not knowing my whereabouts.

"I'm fine now, Grandma. The rangers took me to Weaver House Sanctuary and nursed me. Oh, and I have so many new friends! Orville, Mango, Flo, Little Horn, Ben, Monty, Zizi–"

"Stop, little girl!" said Grandpa, laughing. "That's a lot to take in all at once!" Grandpa hadn't aged but then he had always looked old to me.

"Wait until you meet them," I said excitedly. "Mango, the orangutan, can cook and make hats!"

"Goodness me, this Weaver House does sound like a strange place!" said Grandpa.

"You'll love it," I told him. "And everyone wants to come to your school."

"Well, now that's a different matter altogether," he replied proudly.

"I didn't know animals played football, Buffy," said my father.

"Good exercise for them. It builds muscles, improves coordination, teaches them attack and defence strategies, and, best of all, team spirit."

"Excellent," Papa agreed.

"Plus, it helps the little ones from the sanctuary forget their woes for a while," he whispered to my father.

Papa nodded approvingly.

"Can we stay and watch please, Papa?" asked Winkle.

"Of course, we all will."

"You can help me with the scoring," said Buffy, peering down at my baby sister. "Remember the rules, and no cheating like last time, Gussy!" He stared at one of the hippos, rather sternly.

"We'll cheer you on," said the elders.

The game was fast and furious, and it was 5-5 when Gussy picked the ball up in his mouth and ran the length of the field with it.

"That's cheating!" said Monty, showing him a yellow card.

Gussy immediately dropped the ball, allowing Zizi to dribble it down the length of the pitch and score another goal. Little Horn then kicked the ball down towards our end and headed it into the goal.

Gussy intercepted the ball with his nose and, thinking that no one could see, popped it in his mouth again. Monty, however, was keeping up with him and held up a card.

"Red card!" said Monty, waving it in the air excitedly.

"Disqualified! That is not *team spirit*!" bellowed Buffy.

The game was soon over, and with the other team having one hippo down, my side won easily: 10-6.

"Well played everyone, go and cool off in the river and we'll keep an eye on you," promised Buffy.

Gussy swam away in disgrace, while his siblings swam around in circles and discussed tactics for the next match. We preferred to stay on the bank as the big hippos were too close for comfort and everyone knew that this was a popular spot for crocodiles.

"We were worried you might have become a poacher's

snack when you didn't come home," said Papa, nestling in close to me.

"Papa, I'm so sorry Truffle got caught; it was all my fault for not watching properly. I was counting the little five instead."

"No, it wasn't your fault, Happiness; lions are skilled hunters."

"So you saw the little five, Happiness?" smiled Grandma proudly.

I nodded enthusiastically. "All five!"

"We'd best be getting home now," said Mama. "Come along, you can give me all your news on the way."

"I can't come yet, Mama," I said, glancing at my new friends. "Peter helped me, so I must help him in return, mustn't I? Like Zulu helped Truffle."

"You are right," said Grandpa, nodding. "One good turn deserves another. Come home when you are ready, then."

"Thank you," I said happily. "I love you all so much."

Mama rubbed snouts with me very gently and lovingly. "Promise you'll be home soon?"

"Yes, Mama, once my work is done."

My family all said their goodbyes, and I watched as they made their way home without me. I suddenly felt very grown up and rather important.

Happiness and Truffle

Chapter 10

Help is at Hand

Baby Crocodiles

"One, two, three, four, five, six, seven. Seven, yes, seven eggs – yum," counted Monty intently.

"What? Where?" asked Zizi, looking alarmed.

"Look! There. In the sand, right by your feet. Careful, you nearly stepped on them!"

"They're crocodile's eggs!" Zizi leapt into the air with fright.

"They'll be Sugarsnap's eggs," said Buffy, noticing an enormous crocodile emerging from her hiding place. "Hello, old friend. When are they due?"

"Now," nodded the expectant mother, opening her powerful jaws and exposing her sharp, jagged teeth. "They started calling to me this morning." She dipped her lower jaw into the sand and scooped the eggs carefully into her mouth.

"I'm taking them into the river to hatch." With that, she slid silently in, keeping her head just above the waterline.

We watched in fascination as tiny fractures appeared in the eggshells and her hatchlings tapped their way out using their little noses and slipped out between the gaps in her teeth to take their first swim.

"Congratulations!" said Buffy.

"Thank you," she grinned. "By the way, Buffy, you might like to tell Peter that the poachers are back. I've been watching them from my hideout. Just give me the nod and I'll eat them. Come on babies, time for a nap." She scooped them back into her mouth and swaggered off, down the bank. The newborns' watery eyes peeped out innocently from between her pointed teeth.

Just then, a very fat male hippopotamus heaved himself out of the river and shook river water from his whiskers. He stank.

"I overheard Sugarsnap and I want to help too," he said in a voice even gruffer then Buffy's. "The poachers are putting our lives at risk by coming up and down our river in their speedboats. Our wives are busy having babies underwater, and the other day an engine blade killed a newborn."

"I'm so sorry to hear that, Hoppo," said Buffy, lowering his head in respect. "I'll pass on the sad news to the rangers this evening."

"Thanks, mate. Oh, and if you bump into Hugo, tell him his mother's looking for him." Wading back into the river, Hoppo sank underwater, leaving a halo of bubbles on the surface.

I'd been watching this whole exchange thoughtfully. Now there were two more animals to help me with my plan.

With thundering hooves and a cloud of dust Mr and Mrs Twiga screeched to a halt in front of Buffy.

"Please help us, we're desperate, Buffy! You know our son Twig, don't you? Well, he went missing yesterday. He does it from time to time but never for this long. We've looked everywhere but we can't find him anywhere!" Mrs Twiga was frantic.

"Have you called out his name, Mrs Twiga?" suggested Flo.

"Of course not, you daft bird. You know he's stone deaf," replied Mr Twiga rather sharply. "We sent messages by stamping the ground, but we've had no reply from him… it's most unusual."

"Sorry, I forgot. I'll fetch Orville and we'll fly over the reserve and look for him," said Flo apologetically.

"Don't worry, he'll turn up. Come home with us, Mr and Mrs Twiga; Orville and Flo will bring us news when they've found him," invited Buffy to the fraught parents.

As we turned to leave, a small voice called out. "Help, help, Buffy, it's me! Please, wait!"

A young, embarrassed baby hippo emerged from a bush, absolutely covered in brown sludge and green cabbage leaves.

Hugo

"Ah, there you are, Hugo," said Buffy, staring down at the tubby youngster. "What on earth have you been up to? Your mother's worried sick *and* you missed the football match."

"I was playing 'hold your breath' with the others and I closed my eyes to concentrate. When I opened them again the current had carried me down the river. I've only just found my way back," he sobbed.

"The others are over there," said Buffy, nodding towards them. "Now run along."

Relieved, Hugo trotted off happily with his little tail swinging from side to side.

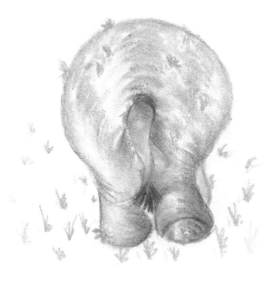

Hugo's Bottom

"Thank you, Buffy," he blubbed. "I promise I won't do it again."

With Hugo safely reunited with his family, we started to make our way back and it was almost dark by the time we reached home.

"Look who's here!" said Peggy busily filling all our food bowls.

To everyone's relief, it was young Twig – safe and sound.

"Where did you find him?" asked his mother, rushing over to her son.

"Wandering round and round in circles in the woods," said Flo. "Luckily, his head poked out above the trees."

"I spotted him first," muttered Orville.

The three giraffes wrapped their necks together and gazed at each other lovingly from under their thick eyelashes.

"What happened?" asked Mrs Twiga, releasing her neck. "Didn't you feel us stamping? We stamped out dozens of messages!"

After studying her lips carefully, Twig replied, "I'm so sorry! I wandered too far to pick up the signals; I promise I won't ever do it again."

Mr Twiga unwrapped his neck too. "Thank you, Orville. Thank you, Flo. Thank you all so much. You must promise to let us know if there is anything we can ever do for you," he concluded.

"I promise," I assured him, mentally adding them to my list of helpers.

The family made a slow and graceful exit and Mango closed the gates for the night.

"Peggy, have you heard? Have you heard the news?" Monty bounced up and down on the spot. "Happy has found her family! Happy has found her family!"

"Yes, I heard from Flo. It's truly wonderful news, Happiness, but I hope you won't leave just yet, we're getting rather fond of you."

"No, I won't, as a matter of fact. I'll stay a little longer, if I may?"

"As long as you like, dear."

I thanked Buffy for a lovely day out and ate my supper quickly. I was exhausted and went to bed early. I had so much to think about. It was definitely time to hatch a plan. I dragged my snack basket close by in case I needed a nibble in the night and closed my eyes.

With an elephant, a crocodile, a hippo, a buffalo, a lion and some giraffes willing to help now, we could surely catch the poachers.

Twig

Chapter 11

A New Arrival

I overslept and woke to find the others had already gone downstairs but Peggy was busy preparing a new bed in the nursery corner of our dormitory, kept especially for sick or injured baby animals. I was curious to know whom it might be for but I didn't say anything as I could see she'd been crying.

"Morning dear, I let you sleep because you were so tired."

"Thank you, Peggy, I feel much better now *and* I've got a plan to catch the poachers!"

"Oh Happiness, it would be wonderful if you could. Peter and Harry are bringing another casualty home today. I can hear the truck, they must be back already!" We quickly went down, Mango swung the gates open and the truck rolled slowly to a stop just in front of us.

My name is Happiness

Peter and Harry jumped out of their seats looking very distraught. They went round the back and carefully let the ramp down. Peter's dogs pushed past and went to drink hurriedly from the pond. Orville flew silently off his perch on the truck and watched from his branch above.

Little Horn sensed something was wrong and began to tremble. He pressed himself firmly against me for comfort. Monty and Ben ran up Zizi's legs and sat huddled side by side on his back.

We couldn't see what was inside but Harry was trying his hardest to encourage it out with kind words. Peter tiptoed up the ramp and tried to give it a nudge.

After several minutes the animal made its way cautiously down the ramp and when we saw what it was we all gasped. It was a newborn calf elephant, far too young to be without its parents. So very young that its head was still covered with a cap of dark baby hair. Huge tears rolled down her floppy, limp trunk, each one landing with a plop at her trembling feet.

Peter and Harry walked either side of her to help her feel protected. They led her up to the corner of the tree house to the bed that Peggy had prepared. Little Horn, Zizi and I tiptoed quietly behind.

The calf's knees gave way, and she crumpled onto the soft

pile of fresh grass, closing her eyes. We just stood there and stared at her, unsure of how to console her. Something terrible must have happened. Ben, who is not afraid of elephants like mice are, crept quietly up to the tip of her trunk and kissed it gently.

"Hello, my name is Ben. I cried when I came here too, but you're safe now. We'll be your friends and I'll look after you. What's your name?"

She slowly opened her big, brown eyes and looked at him before glancing over at Little Horn who stood just beside him. When she saw the rhino's bright pink handkerchief, she blinked several times and a tiny smile appeared at the corners of her mouth for just a split second.

"Thank you," she said quietly. "My name is Kili, but I don't feel like talking now."

"Excuse me, but Peggy says she's got to drink this," whispered Mango, appearing with a bottle of milk in his hand.

"She's too sad," said Ben, frowning.

"I know, but Peggy said she must. It's mixed with honey and herbs for shock," insisted Mango.

Kili looked at Mango with astonishment: she had probably never seen an orangutan before, let alone one in a hat.

"No, thank you, what a funny place this is. I want to go home. I want my mummy," she muttered helplessly.

Ben tilted his small, soft head to one side, lifted her ear with his tiny paw and whispered into it.

After a few moments, she replied, "If I must," before clutching the bottle feebly in her trunk.

Once she had finished sucking, Mango suggested we leave her alone for a while to sleep. "We'll be back soon. Get some rest. Ben, you stay with her."

The calf closed her eyes and Ben curled up inside the bend of her tiny trunk.

"What happened, Peter?" I asked when we were out of earshot.

"Where did you find her, Harry?" asked Mango.

"Orville spotted a helicopter landing on the far side of the reserve. We saw Solo's father, Eddie, and his herd stampeding, but by the time we reached the scene of the crime, Kili's grandfather, Jumbo, was dead, and the poachers had taken off in a helicopter with his tusks."

He blew his nose loudly into a large handkerchief and wiped his tears away with the back of his hand. "The calf was in shock and hadn't moved so I called Peggy and suggested we bring her here for now."

"How awful," said Little Horn, crying. "Where are her parents?"

"They'll be hiding in the woods." Peter shook his head. "These poachers are very cunning; they're always one step ahead of us. It's as if they know something before we do. It's like they have a mole."

"A mole!" said Mango incredulously. "But you don't get moles in Africa!"

"He means a spy in the camp," said Orville, "not the underground kind with sharp teeth and pointy noses. A mole is someone who tells tales like they do in wars. A sneak."

"I have an inkling who it might b– b– b– be," offered Spike. "I've often seen that sm– sm– sm– smelly skunk, Stinkers, creeping around. Perhaps he gives them inside information!"

"*In-side in-for-ma-tion!*" repeated Mango.

"He's t-t-totally untrustworthy," continued Spike. "In fact, I've actually overheard him tell the p– p– p– poachers where to find rhinos and elephants in return for s– s– s– snacks."

"Why on earth didn't you tell us before?" squawked Orville, aghast.

"I didn't th– th– think," said Spike, blushing hotly. "But I know where he h– h– h– hangs out. I pretend to be friends with him so he doesn't make me sm– sm– smelly, 'specially since I've just got married."

Holly gave him a quick kiss on the nose and flattened her spines in a most feminine way.

"This could be very helpful," said Harry. "We can feed him information," he suggested.

"Excuse me, everyone," I coughed politely, "but I have a plan."

"A plan?" said Harry and Peter in unison.

"Yes, a plan to catch the poachers!" I cleared my throat. "If you and Peter dig a large pit, Buffy and the bull can carry the dug soil into the woods and scatter it. Then we must cover the pit so the poachers can't see it and warn everyone on the reserve of its whereabouts."

"I'll see to that," volunteered Orville.

"I've got some strong netting you can use to cover it," offered Peggy.

"But what's the pit for?" asked Little Horn.

"To catch the poachers in," I explained. "We have to lure them towards it and I know just the animal for the job!"

"Who?" asked Little Horn, panicking.

"Solo, the lonely elephant. If he does a good deed then his father Eddie will let him back into the herd. If the poachers are after elephant's tusks, he's perfect bait. His tusks are huge."

"Good plan," said Orville. "But what if they shoot him?"

"Buffy and Zulu can stand guard, and we'll make sure he is just out of reach. After all, Zulu said he was on our side too."

I turned to Flo. "We'll need lookouts. I need you to fly down to the river and ask Sugarsnap the crocodile and Hoppo the hippo to patrol the river in case they come by boat and if they do to tip them out and keep them as prisoners on the bank."

"And I'll hide my boat and wait there too," offered Harry.

"Thanks, Harry. Please, also ask Twig and his parents to patrol the woods in case the poachers come by truck. And, if they do, to warn us as soon as possible. Orville, please find Solo and Zulu, and ask them to go and wait at the pit tomorrow."

"Why don't Peter or Harry just shoot them?" asked Monty naively.

"You can't go around shooting people. They've got families too," I pointed out.

"But *they* shoot elephants and rhinos," Monty insisted.

"It's illegal and wrong," I said, "and that's why we must stop them. Two wrongs don't make a right."

"Let's give it a try, then," encouraged Harry, rubbing his hands together enthusiastically. "Where shall we dig?" He plucked a crumpled map from his pocket. "How about here?" he said, jabbing it with his finger. "Under the buffalo thorn tree, so it can't be seen from the sky and over on this side of Thorny Wood. The poachers will never walk through those dense trees, so they can only come from one direction."

"What if they come in a helicopter?" asked Mango.

"I'll tell you later," I whispered back.

"What's the exact position and map reference?" enquired Flo, fluffing up her feathers.

"Map reference, forty-nine degrees west and twenty-seven degrees south of here," said Harry. "Flo, Orville and Spike, have you all got that?"

"Yes," replied Orville, spreading his wings in preparation.

"Yes. Forty-nine d– d– degrees west and twenty-seven degrees s– s– s– south," said Spike, spanning his quills.

"Tell Stinkers that Solo will be taking his supper there tomorrow evening. Then we just have to hope that the poachers come back and that our plan falls into place."

"Are you sure you know what you are doing?" queried Holly, trying to keep up with Spike.

"Of c– c– course I do" he retorted, striding ahead.

When Mango opened the gates to let the porcupines out, Solo, Buffy and Zulu happened to be on the other side, waiting to come in.

"Your ears must be burning," said Harry. "Right on cue!"

Solo flapped his huge ears and checked them with the tip of his trunk to make sure they weren't actually on fire. "Why's that?"

"Happiness will explain all."

Zulu lay down and flexed his razor-sharp claws one by one.

"It's a brilliant idea," said Solo. "Definitely get me back into my herd," he said, having listened to my plan.

"Make sure you always keep just out of range," yawned Zulu, "but if they come too close, I'll scare them off."

"Teamwork," commented Buffy. "Better get started."

"Cool," said Harry. "I'll go and fetch the bull."

Zulu

Chapter 12

Kili's Tale

"Uncle Solo, Uncle Solo!" cried out Kili. She stumbled down the ramp with Ben scampering behind her.

"Little Kili!" trumpeted Solo, surprised to see her. "What on earth are you doing here?"

She wrapped her soft, floppy trunk around his thick, bristly ankle and her uncle patted her fluffy head gently with his trunk.

"What's happened?" he asked when she was settled.

"I heard your voice.

Haven't you heard about Grandpa Jumbo?" she blurted out.

"Oh no. Not him as well as Big Horn. Is he dead too?"

Kili nodded and spoke so softly we could barely hear her. "The rangers saved me," she spluttered.

"Take it slowly, Kili. In your own time."

"We were just about to walk to a new feeding area when we heard the sound of a helicopter coming closer and closer, so we hid under the trees, but the blades whirred round and round so fast that it disturbed the branches and we could be seen. They landed not far away and crept towards us as everyone circled around me for protection. We flapped our ears and stamped the ground, and we were just about to charge when a crack rang out and Grandpa Jumbo crashed to the ground. Everyone started to run, but I got dust in my eyes and couldn't see and I couldn't move my feet."

Her uncle stroked her spine gently with the tip of his trunk, trying to soothe her, but the hairs on his back bristled with fury.

"There, there, you're safe now. Little Horn, take her into the pond for a swim, would you?"

Kili perked up at this suggestion and released her uncle's leg. She followed Little Horn into the water, sucked some soft mud up from the bottom of the pond with her trunk and splattered it on her head to make a mud cap.

Flapper waded quietly at the water's edge.

"Hello, you're new. Where are you from?" he asked her.

"Near Mount Kilimanjaro," replied Kili.

"I come from near there too. My wing is better so I'm

heading back tomorrow."

"Flapper, Flapper?" I said quickly, rushing over. "Could you stay on for a couple of days? I need you, Orville and Mango to do something for me, to help catch the poachers."

"Of course, what is it?"

I called Mango over and signalled for Orville to join us. I whispered my instructions to them and they nodded accordingly. I had decided that since we couldn't be sure the poachers would come by boat or vehicle, I needed a Plan B, and since this could be a very dangerous mission, I wanted to keep it as secret as possible.

Just then footsteps approached; it was Harry leading the bull by the nose. The bull pulled a cart full of pickaxes, spades and nets.

"Well, we're ready," said Harry keenly.

"Listen here, everyone," said Peter. "Those of you helping dig the pit must come with us. Orville, Flo and Spike have their orders – the rest of you stay behind. Absolutely NO going out today."

Mango opened the gates. Harry and the bull with his cart, Buffy, Zulu and Solo walked ahead. Peter let me ride in the back of his truck and the others waved us off, wishing us luck.

We found the spot under the buffalo thorn tree without encountering any signs of danger. Solo had made sure to leave some steaming dollops of dung along the path as clues to his whereabouts.

To our delight, my friends from the Chagga tribe were waiting for us under the tree; the chief had heard about my plan from Flo and wanted to help. Peter and Harry were thrilled to have some extra manpower.

It took all day to dig the pit in the sweltering heat. They swung their pickaxes hour after hour, chipping away at the hard topsoil until, finally, they broke through to softer earth. They heaved the soil into the cart and Buffy and the bull hauled it into the woods to be scattered. Finally, the men laid the nets on top and held them down with heavy stones.

"We'll fill it in when you've finished with it," offered the chief. He and his men gathered up their tools and jogged sprightly off into the distance.

Solo made his way over to the far side of the pit, just short of the dense woodland, while Zulu and Buffy chose hiding places close by.

A few seconds later, the voice of General Ant rang out, "Left, right, left, right. HALT!"

"Hello, General," I said.

"Hello, Happy. I heard about this from Flo – jolly good work! There's just one thing, though."

"What?" I asked, suddenly worried.

"I saw some hunters flying over in a helicopter, but they didn't land; they could just be nosing around."

"That means they'll be back! Don't worry, I'm hatching another plan to catch them," I said in hushed tones. "And I'll need your help, please."

I told him what I needed his men to do, and he just laughed and laughed! "Looking forward to it," he said. "It's a grand plan, meet me at the clearing at dawn."

"Hello, General," said Peter. "What's the joke?"

"Oh, nothing important, nothing at all," the General replied. "I just popped by to take some of the spare soil for our new barracks."

"Help yourself; there's plenty of it," said Peter.

"Much obliged."

Each soldier filled a tiny bucket to the brim, patting it down firmly with a small but well-polished foot.

"No time to waste, then. Forward. March!" commanded the General, winking at me.

As we watched the troops march off, weighed down by their loads, Spike and Holly came beetling towards us.

"We've d– d– d– done it," Spike said breathlessly. "We've told st– st– st– Stinkers. He's making his way to the river to wait for the p– p– poachers and tell them where Solo is. If they come that way, that is."

"Thank you, excellent work," said Peter.

"Okay, everyone, that's enough for now. Peggy will be wondering where we are."

Once home we found everyone waiting at the gates desperate for news.

"Hurry up, tell us everything," begged Little Horn.

"Let them eat and drink first," ordered Peggy, handing out supper. "Looks like you men need a cold shower!"

With Peter and Harry out of earshot, I took the opportunity to talk to Orville, Mango and Flapper. "We're going to have to put Plan B into action. General Ant saw men flying a helicopter so let's go out at dawn in case they come over again. But we can't tell Peter and Harry or they won't let us go."

"Mum's the word," said Orville clamping his beak firmly shut.

"Are you sure you want to do this?" I said. "It could be very dangerous."

"You bet," replied Mango.

"Of course," added Flapper.

"Mmmm," nodded Orville.

"If they come in the night I'll wake you, otherwise, I'll see you at dawn," said Mango.

"Let's get some kip," I suggested.

Chapter 13

Flapper's Foil

Flapper

I felt something dig my side. "Is it morning already?" I asked, jumping to my feet.

Flapper stopped poking me and opened his beak. I peered inside his pouch. It was full to the brim with small, sharp stones.

"Take care, Flapper," I whispered. "Promise me."

He nodded since he couldn't speak with such a mouthful, and with much flapping of his graceful wings, he made a slow ascent into the dawn sky.

I met Mango at the gate. He was wearing the outfit he'd been made to wear in the circus and looked just like a real pilot. Orville watched over us as we slipped quietly through the gates without waking any of the others. There was a deathly hush on the reserve since most of the animals were still fast asleep. The nocturnal bats and owls dipped and swooped silently around us.

I was excited and terrified at the same time; so much was at stake.

Finally, we reached the clearing where General Ant had told me to meet him, and Mango and I hid behind a thorny bush to wait. Seeing my nervous expression, he placed a warm hand on my back and gave me a soft, pouty kiss on the snout. We didn't dare speak.

After what seemed like an eternity, the sun rose in the sky and a distant movement caught our attention. It flew closer and closer until the helicopter came straight towards us in full view.

I held my breath; timing was crucial!

I could see one poacher peering out of his window as he

slowed the engine down until the helicopter was hovering right above our heads. Another man pointed the barrel of a gun out of his window. A wire cage had been fixed to the undercarriage to carry their booty.

The blades spun the dry earth around us into a dusty tornado, making it difficult to see, but as the pilot prepared to land, Flapper appeared above them – right on cue – and opened his beak.

The stones dropped from his pouch onto the blades, immediately stalling the engine, and the men screamed as they lost control of the helicopter. It tipped right and then left, spinning speedily round and round in circles before crash-landing in front of us. Feathers floated silently down from above.

The dazed poachers pushed the dented door open and stumbled out, and that's when General Ant shouted, "Now!"

The soldier ants raced towards them. Some ran up their legs and went inside their shorts and pants, pinching and nipping as hard as they could, while other ants went inside the men's shirts.

The men jumped up and down, frantically slapping themselves and yanking at their clothes in a complete frenzy. Dozens of the little five appeared from the undergrowth to watch this spectacle from a safe distance and cheered the ants on.

"We surrender!" screeched one poacher.

"Get them off!" begged the other.

"Only if you swear you will NEVER kill again," ordered the General.

"We can't; we need the money," replied the first, still hopping up and down.

"It's dirty money. If you keep killing, there will be no more rhinos left. No more elephants! Then how will you earn a living? Tell me that!"

"If you get these ants off us, we'll work for the rangers instead!" he cried.

"Enough?" the General asked me.

"For now," I replied.

"Retreat!" shouted the General.

Those that could still walk helped the less able-bodied. Some of the ants had missing legs, and a few dropped to the ground and didn't move.

"We must count the dead and treat the wounded," said the General solemnly, before turning to the men. "We'll deal with you later."

The ants that were too young to be in combat carried tiny stretchers over to the fallen and lifted their colleagues carefully onto them.

The dead were laid down in a row.

"Six fallen soldiers, sir," observed one.

"Some of them have been smacked beyond recognition," declared the General. "Now dig their graves."

"Sergeant, take their ID tags off their necks and tell their families they died in the line of duty."

"Sir."

"I'll dig the graves," offered one of the poachers. "We didn't mean to kill *them*."

Using his thumb, he made six small holes in the shade before gently lowering the bodies in and covering them with soil. Mango plucked some jacaranda flowers off a nearby tree and placed one on the top of each grave.

Ants' graves

In a cloud of dust, a van rumbled up with Orville on the roof and two police officers stepped out.

"Congratulations!" said one of them, slapping me on the back rather hard. "It seems you've been doing our job! How did you know they would be here?"

"Inside information, really; we just got word," I replied.

"*In-side in-for-ma-tion,*" repeated Mango.

The policeman cuffed the poachers and shoved them into the prison van.

"Congratulations! Who would have thought it? What a wily little pig you are!" said the Chief Officer.

"What will you do with the helicopter, sir?" asked Mango.

"You can keep it. None of us knows how to fly one," replied

the chief. "I'm sure Harry would like to learn! It would be very useful on the reserve."

"Without that, we're definitely out of a job!" muttered one of the prisoners, staring forlornly at the helicopter through the bars of the van.

"Wow! Thank you very much. I know how to fly one. Can I fly it home?" said Mango. Without waiting for an answer, he pulled himself up into the cockpit and with much chattering of teeth and fiddling with knobs, he pulled on a stopper and the engine burst into life.

"Come on, Happiness, climb aboard!" he yelled.

"Yippee!" I exclaimed.

"In you get."

The policeman lifted me in next to Mango and closed the damaged door. Up we went, soaring higher and higher. Orville flew alongside winking and blinking, his wings moving faster than usual in order to keep up with us.

It was the most incredible feeling, gazing down at the reserve. Most of the animals were still asleep, but those that weren't looked up in amazement as we flew over.

I could just about see my den, and while it was pretty much just a grubby hole, it was still my home. As I looked down at the top of the buffalo thorn tree, I could see the tip of Solo's trunk nibbling on a branch. I closed my eyes and made a wish. I wished as hard as I could that we could save all animals from poaching forever and ever.

Mango flew us home just like a real pilot and we landed safely in the garden. Flapper had beaten us to it and had already told the animals about the ambush. They were all terribly excited and ran round and round the helicopter to inspect it.

Peggy, however, was not pleased – she was clearly very upset. "Come here, Happiness, and look what you've done to Flapper." She was gently dabbing the inside of his beak pouch. "His wing's broken again and his mouth's badly cut. *And* half his feathers are missing! That was a risky thing you did, Happiness," she said, shaking her head.

"I'm so sorry," I whimpered. "I didn't mean anyone to get hurt. We did it because we had to."

"Sometimes you must think with your head, not your heart. What if one of you had got shot?" she asked, glaring at me.

"I had to help, Peggy," I tried to explain. "Please, don't be cross with me. I saw our wonderful homes from the sky. Imagine a world without elephants and rhinos. Or, or lions, or even warthogs?"

"I know, dearest Happy," she replied more calmly, "but I was so worried when I found your bed empty and didn't know where you were. Peter and Harry have been driving all over looking for you." Leaning down, she gave me a bear hug. "Thank goodness you're all safe," she whispered.

Peter stormed over to me – he was absolutely livid. "What on earth were you thinking, going out there on your own?" he shouted.

"Orville was keeping an eye out," I said, trying to defend my actions.

"What you did was very dangerous and could have cost you all your lives. You should have told Harry and me."

My name is Happiness

I fought back tears. I wanted to show them that I could help, but instead, everyone was just angry and disappointed in me. "I'm sorry," I said, my voice trembling. "When I heard what happened to Little Horn's and Kili's families, I had to do something."

"I understand your reason," said Peter, "but don't take any more stupid risks. Promise? Now go and rest and don't leave here again without my permission."

I slunk off to my bed to hide away, feeling very deflated and humiliated, and Hebe followed me up.

"I think you're very brave and very clever," she told me. "Mum and Dad were just worried that you might have got hurt, but they'll calm down soon. They are actually very proud of you. Just have a nap, you must be exhausted."

She kissed me gently on the head, and with these soothing words ringing in my ears, I drifted off to sleep and slept all day.

Chapter 14

Another Ambush

Monty

My name is Happiness

Orville gave me a gentle peck on the nose. "Wake up – time to go." It was getting dark but the moon shone brightly enough for us to see.

Peter had already packed his rucksack with supplies in case we had a long wait: meat for Zulu, bananas for Solo and seed cake for me. Zizi and Monty insisted on coming since they had "missed out on all the fun earlier" as Monty put it, and they promised to blend in and act naturally.

Orville informed me that Harry had already left to join the others at the riverbank. Flo would sit on a branch close by and send him messages if needed and watch out for any signs from Twig and his parents.

Peggy and Hebe came to wave us off.

"Good luck and promise to come back safely!"

Mango blew us kisses and locked the gates behind us.

Peter and I set off in the truck while Zizi and Monty followed discreetly behind – Monty as always, cadging a ride on Zizi's back.

Once close to the pit, Peter hid the truck in the woods and then we made our way on foot. When we reached the others he quietly threw them their snacks and they silently nodded their thanks.

Peter and I moved into our hideouts – each choosing a bush that fitted our size. Orville perched high up in a tree turning his head in full circles, on constant watch and ready for action at a moment's notice. Zizi and Monty melted into the background.

There was nothing to do now but wait.

From time to time, one of Flo's friends would flit past, shaking their heads, but apart from that, it was still and silent.

Everyone on the reserve knew by now what was about to happen and was keeping out of the way.

When I had just about given up hope, Flo flew in, shaking like a leaf. She could hardly speak.

"What's happened?" I whispered.

Once she'd composed herself she told us that the boat had moored as expected, except that there were four men on board, not the anticipated two, which was more usual. Sugarsnap and Hoppo had risen out of the water and scared them inland, and they were now heading our way.

"That's good news," said Orville, putting his reassuring wing around Flo's shoulders to comfort her.

"Yes, but that's not all," she chattered. It turned out that Gussy – the naughty hippo who had been told quite firmly by his father to keep away – wanted to help, and in his enthusiasm had accidentally tipped Harry's boat over, trapping him underneath. With much pushing and heaving, Hoppo had righted the boat and Harry had clawed his way to the bank. Sugarsnap had ordered all her newborns to jump on his back repeatedly until all the water in his lungs had been coughed up.

"Shhh, everyone hide!" squawked Orville. "They're coming this way!"

Sure enough, we could hear not only their footsteps but also the four men arguing among themselves!

"How do you know it's not a trap?" said one of them.

"Trap? Don't be stupid," said a second.

"Well, why were the hippo and croc waiting for us, then?" questioned a third.

"Waiting for us?" asked a fourth. "Those dumb animals aren't intelligent enough to think! Anyway, I'm not going back until I've got the tusks, and I'll take the crocodile's skin, too, for that matter. I'd like some new shoes."

"Don't call me stupid," said number one, a little slow with his come-back.

"Shut up!" hissed number two, before adding, "Look, Stinkers was very precise about the elephant's location, so let's just kill the beast and take his tusks. We've lost our boat so we'll have to wait for the others to airlift us out of here."

"They were meant to be in the clearing we just passed. I wonder where they are," said number three.

"They'll turn up! Just stop fussing and shut your trap," snapped number four.

"I've got a bad feeling about this," said number two. "In fact, I think I need the loo; all that excitement has upset me."

"Oh for goodness' sake," said number one, exasperated. "Hurry up and go in the bushes!"

As it happened, he chose my bush to go in, and just as he pulled down his shorts, I dug my tiny tusks firmly into his bare buttocks.

"Yeeouch!" he yelled at the top of his lungs.

"What on earth is going on?" hissed number one under his breath.

"Some blasted pig was in the bush!" gasped number two, who was still trying to catch his breath.

"Pull yourself together, you fool!" said number one between clenched teeth.

"Don't you call me a fool!" retorted number two, making a fist with one hand and yanking his shorts up with the other. When he was dressed again, he threw a punch towards number one's chin, but as he ducked out of the way, it landed on number three's mouth instead and knocked several teeth out.

"I should never have brought you lot along on my shoot," spluttered number three, wiping blood off his cheek. "Take this!" he added and waved a clenched fist at anyone who got in his way.

"It's not your hunt: it's mine," said number four.

"No, it's mine!" replied at least two of the others.

By this time, they had dropped their guns and were swinging punches left, right and centre, and cursing and swearing as loudly as they could.

I was trying hard not to laugh when I saw Zulu creep up on them. Buffy backed into the trees.

"What have we here? Four delicious-looking snacks, plenty for *all* the family!" purred Zulu.

The hunters raised their hands above their heads.

"Please don't eat us," begged number one, sweat dripping from his brow.

"Why not?" asked Zulu, sharpening his claws on a tree trunk.

"We're going to kill a huge elephant," said number two desperately. "We only want the tusks, so you can eat the body!"

"I see. How very generous of you," said Zulu licking his lips. "What an excellent plan. Well, you're in luck: there's a particularly large elephant just over there, standing in a moonbeam."

He let them pick up their guns, but he added, "Don't try anything funny; I'm watching you."

Zulu slunk after them, and we crept after him, keeping a good distance between us. Peter crouched down with his gun at the ready.

The men stopped mere centimetres from the edge of the pit. Number four actually rested his foot on one of the stones holding the netting in place.

"He's flipping enormous!" observed number three, tightening the silencer on his shotgun as he stared at Solo. Squinting down the barrel he added, "I'll get the blasted lion, too, when I've done this one in!"

Solo was magnificent. He stood tall, proud and fearless, munching nonchalantly on a branch. So confident that the plan would work, he turned his head and waved his trunk at them. Then he turned his back on them and strolled into the dense woods, cool as a cucumber.

"Blast it," said number three. "Come on, let's go after him!"

The four men broke into a run, charging straight into the pit and causing the net to collapse neatly on top of them. The more they struggled, the tighter it became. Their guns became completely entangled so were now useless weapons.

Everyone gathered around and stared down at them.

"I can't believe it worked!" exclaimed Peter.

"You can come out now, Solo," roared Zulu.

Our hero emerged from the woods, raised his trunk to the sky and trumpeted like he'd never trumpeted before. In the distance, another elephant replied.

"Father Eddie says I can come home!" announced Solo.

Monty ran up his leg and sat behind his ears. "Three cheers for Solo!" he said, as everyone joined in:

"Hip hip hooray! Hip hip hooray! Hip hip hooray!"

Blushing heavily, Solo modestly lowered his head just as the same police officers from yesterday morning pulled up next to us all and jumped out of their van.

"Congratulations, Happiness! Six poachers in one day! If you can keep this up, I'll make you head of police! Sergeant, confiscate the guns, then get the men and handcuff them."

They lowered a ladder down for the criminals to climb up. When they were out of the pit, they were handcuffed, bundled into the police van and locked behind a grille.

"May I have a word with them before you leave, sir?" I asked.

"Be my guest," said the chief.

I walked over to the van and spoke through the grille. "You are very bad, greedy men; shame on you for killing helpless animals for money."

"It's the only way we can make a living," said the one who seemed to be the ringleader. The others nodded in agreement.

"But if you keep killing them, there will be none left. Don't you see?"

"I don't care. It's good money," replied the man, shrugging.

"You will care, once you've been to Peter's school!" I said. "We'll turn you into good men; just you wait and see!"

They started to laugh at me then, so the chief came over and closed the doors on them.

"Happiness, they won't laugh at you again. Don't you worry."

I nodded at him, hoping he was right. It felt horrid being laughed at.

"If you don't mind, I'd like to join my herd now." Solo excused himself and swaggered off, humming happily.

"Me too, better get back to the wife and cubs," growled Zulu.

"Thanks, guys! Thanks for your help," I called after them.

"Congratulations, Happiness. You're very clever and I'm proud of you."

"Thank you, Peter. I'm so relieved it worked."

"That was so exciting!" squeaked Monty. "I've never seen real poachers before and they're going to a real prison!"

"Yeah, that was cool, Happiness, really cool. You can save my skin any day!" said Zizi, kicking her back legs in the air.

"Thanks, everyone, but it was a team effort."

"I'm proud of you too," said Buffy, "but I'm old and tired so

I'm off to bed. See you all tomorrow."

"Peter, we'd better go home and see how Harry is. I'll fly on ahead," hooted Orville.

Peter popped me in the back of his truck and started the engine. I trembled from head to trotters with adrenaline and over-excitement. Monty ran up Zizi's leg and onto her back, chanting, "Happy caught the poachers, Happy caught the poachers!"

All along the way, creatures lined our route home, cheering and thanking us for making the reserve a safer place. I wasn't sure whether to laugh or cry, so I did a bit of both.

Everyone was at the gates to greet us. Hebe ran over and gave me a huge bear hug. "Congratulations! Orville's told us everything!" she exclaimed, beaming from ear to ear.

"Well done, Happy, that was awesome!" said Harry, drying his wet hair with a towel.

"Are you okay, Harry?"

"I'm fine thanks, Happy, just sorry to have missed seeing the catch."

It was all too much for Kili. She burst into tears. "Thank you, Happy. Thank you so much. Can I please go home now?"

"Not yet, little one. Solo will come and fetch you tomorrow," promised Harry.

"Kili, please, stay here with me a bit longer," begged Ben. Kili and the bushbaby had bonded and had become very close to each other. Kili scooped him up in her little trunk and popped him onto her head.

"We'll stick together," she promised him.

"We must celebrate," said Peggy, handing glasses to Harry and Peter and a small bowl to me.

"Champagne! A toast to our ingenious friend, Happiness the heroine."

"Toast?" Monty giggled.

"To Happiness!" said Harry, raising his glass in the air.

I took a sip from my bowl and the bubbles tickled my snout.

"Thank you, but does anyone mind if I go to bed?" I asked. Exhaustion had just come over me and I simply had to lie down.

"Don't you want any supper?" said Mango with a mouthful.

"I'm too tired and I think the champagne has gone to my head!"

"Me too," said Monty stifling a yawn, "I'm tired after all the excitement but we'll all sleep safer in our beds tonight."

Mango, Zizi, Monty, Kili, Ben and Little Horn followed me up and we all snuggled up together, except for Mango who climbed into his nest with some bananas and peanuts.

"Your lucky charm works," whispered Little Horn. "I only hope that mine does, too, one day."

"It's going to be a full moon tomorrow," said Mango, looking up at the sky through the tiny gap in the roof. He lay back with his hands behind his head and closed his eyes. "I've got an idea." None of us heard what his idea was because we were already asleep.

Part III

Birthday Celebrations

Chapter 15

Party Plans

"Wake up, everybody, time to get up," tweeted Flo.

"I've just checked the weather and it's going to be a clear night tonight and a full moon," Orville hooted.

"Listen, Mango, it's going to be a full moon tonight. It's your third birthday and my second!" I exclaimed excitedly.

"And my first," added Little Horn, still a little sleepy.

"And mine," added Kili, waggling her trunk.

"Can it be mine too?" piped up Ben.

"And mine, please," implored Monty.

"Of course, we can all celebrate together," I said. "We *must* have a party. Let's go and find Peggy and Hebe; they'll have to help us plan it."

We raced downstairs excitedly, gathering Flapper, Spike

and Holly along the way. Twig and Hugo had come to play so they joined our procession to Weaver House. Flo and Orville flew ahead and the rest of us raced up the ramp into the sitting room. Twig, being so tall, had to stay outside along with Hugo who reluctantly admitted that he was too smelly to go inside. Twig put his head through an upstairs window to watch what was going on inside the house and Ben promised to relay the goings on.

"Peggy, Peggy, please, can you make a humongous birthday cake?" asked Mango, bursting into the kitchen.

"Why, whose birthday is it?" she replied, wiping her hands on her apron.

"All of ours!" we shouted.

"Well, I never!" Peggy exclaimed. "Whom will you invite?"

"Everybody! Every man, woman and beast on the reserve," enthused Monty.

Ben relayed the news to Twig, mouthing every word slowly enough for Twig to lip-read, and Twig then passed the news on to Hugo. Hugo was so overexcited at the thought of a party that he spun round and round in circles until he was quite dizzy.

"Except snakes and scorpions," continued Monty.

"Or spiders," added Ben, "they scare me."

"I think everyone should come to the party, big or small, hairy or scary," said Kili innocently. "It's a peace party."

"I agree, Kili, there should be no exceptions but snakes and scorpions can be unpredictable so I think we'll leave them out. How *do* you know it's your birthday, Mango?" asked Peggy, amused by all the commotion.

"Because it's a full moon," he explained.

"But there are thirteen full moons every year," said Hebe, laughing.

Peggy shushed her. "I'll ring all of my friends and ask them to help with food," she suggested.

"I can fly over the reserve and invite everyone," offered Orville. "I think anyone living at Weaver House can have as many guests as they want, but the rest will be limited to four per family, otherwise it will be mayhem! Shall we invite the villagers and their children?"

"Of course, Orville. Children absolutely make a party, and Hebe and Harry must ask some of their friends too," confirmed Peggy.

"Then of course we'll need a band for dancing," chimed Hebe.

"But what games shall we play? We must have party games," shouted Hugo from below, calming down a little.

"Why don't we choose one each?" I suggested, trying to be fair.

Everyone agreed, and after much discussion, Hebe carefully wrote down a list of games alongside the name of the animal that chose it.

PARTY GAMES
1. Running Races – Zizi.
2. Obstacle Course – Monty.
3. Dressing Up Competition – Mango.
4. Pass-the-Parcel – Ben.

5. Friendly Football Match – Little Horn.
6. Guess My Height – Twig.
7. Guess My Weight – Hugo.
8. Guess the Number of Quills – Spike and Holly.
9. Lucky Dip – Kili.
10. Treasure Hunt – Orville and Flo.
11. How Many Stones Can I Fit In My Beak? – Flapper.
12. Hide-and-Seek – Happy.

The list was complete and Hebe asked if any of us wanted to dress up.

"Me, me, me!" called Mango, Kili, Zizi and Little Horn.

"Can I have a birthday hat?" asked Mango.

Hebe nodded. "Let's start with you, then."

He patted his head with both hands – a sure sign of heightened excitement – and they got down to work.

The whole day was a flurry of activity. Harry measured Twig and weighed Hugo, Peter marked out a racetrack and a football pitch, Flo volunteered to decorate the tables and chairs and disappeared for hours to gather decorations, Peggy hung candle lanterns from the trees and tied balloons to the gates, and our friendly local flamingos offered to line the path on both sides to add some colour and grace to the entrance.

Peggy's friends arrived throughout the day, loaded down with plates of food, and helped prepare pass-the-parcel and the lucky dip. Even the queen bee flew in with her workers and left small bowls of honey and beeswax candles. In the afternoon, Flo flew in with dozens of beautiful butterflies in attendance;

she asked them to sit down at the centre of the tables and take turns to display their wing patterns.

As the party planning seemed to be under control, I went off in search of Hebe and Mango.

"Don't come in!" Mango screeched, quickly hiding something behind his back but not before I saw it was his birthday hat.

"You're ready, Mango," said Hebe. "Now call Little Horn, Zizi and Kili, please; it's time to get them ready."

Zizi was first. Hebe brushed her coat until it gleamed, and using fine red ribbons, plaited her mane and tail throughout with them. Monty had come to watch so she tried to brush his tail, but he just wouldn't sit still.

"I give up on you, Monty. Come along, Kili, let's make you look pretty for your parents."

Kili sidled up. Hebe gently stroked her trunk and reassured her that she was completely safe at Weaver House and she would soon be reunited with her parents. Then Hebe took out some special animal chalks and drew pretty swirling patterns and flowers all over Kili's face and body. Mango thought she looked so pretty that he took her to a mirror to see for herself.

"Oh my goodness, I've only ever seen myself reflected in water before. I look quite different. What if my parents don't recognise me?"

"They'll recognise you, darling. A parent always knows its baby."

Next, she tied a multicoloured birthday hankie round Little Horn's neck and told him how handsome he looked.

"Now, it's your turn, Happiness," she said, turning to me and smiling.

"Me?" I asked. "I don't think I like dressing up."

To my amazement, she unrolled a little coat with bobbles around the edges, placed it across my back and tied it fast with a ribbon under my tummy.

"Don't blush, darling," exclaimed Hebe. "You look adorable!"

"Fabuloso!" agreed Mango, "and now for my birthday hat!" He plonked it on his head and made a deep bow. It was made from locally grown, organic woven cotton with a thick, dark brown band stitched around the crown. The band had small pockets with Velcro fasteners. From one of these he plucked some folded paper money and from another he took out some peanuts. "It's our IN-VEN-TION," he chattered. "Hebe's and mine – a hat with useful pockets and we're going to sell hundreds and make lots of money for the animals!"

"It's very smart," said Peggy, coming out of the kitchen. "But why have you made a hat with pockets?"

"To keep special things safe of course!"

"Well, you all look wonderful," admired Peggy. "Now, it's time Hebe and I got our party dresses on! By the way, the birthday cake is ready but no peeking, *and* I've left the kitchen clean and tidy, Mango."

Mango didn't reply but he made a mental note to tidy up his mess the next time he made ice cream.

Chapter 16

The Full Moon Party

It was 6 p.m. and the party was about to start. We made our way down to the garden, being careful not to get dirty. The farm piglets ran around squealing with excitement. A lively five-piece steel band started playing in one corner and everyone was suddenly in the party mood.

Peter banged the dinner gong three times. "The guests are coming; go and greet them!"

Mango swung the gates open. The flamingos had lined themselves either side of the path leading up to the gates and the pretty candle lanterns flickered in the trees.

The first guests to arrive were the Chagga tribe, closely followed by dozens of local families from surrounding villages.

"I don't expect any of my family will come," said Buffy

glumly. "And Zulu said he'll be a bit late, but I'm determined to have a good time anyway!"

"Mine couldn't make it in time either, delayed by bad weather apparently," said Mango.

Next came my family; my brothers and sister were in such a hurry to see me again that they pushed and shoved and had to be told to behave by Papa.

"Happy!" giggled Winkle. "Look at you! You're a pig in a blanket!"

"Now, now, stop teasing. She looks very pretty," admired my mother, circling around me and sniffing my coat.

Sugarsnap waddled past, carrying her babies in her jaw. Their little glassy eyes peeped out excitedly from between her teeth. Mr and Mrs Twiga and Twig strolled gracefully in, unlike Hoppo and his pongy, unruly children, who charged in without even saying hello. Gazelles sprang, ostriches ran, aardvarks snuffled and porcupines scuttled. Monkeys swung, raptors glided and water birds waded.

Never before had so many birds and animals on the reserve come together in peace and unity at the same time but with so much food on offer, there was no need to squabble.

The General's army arrived in an orderly fashion, having recovered from their battle the day before. Zizi, Monty, Ben, Spike, Holly and Flo greeted their various relatives and offered them food and drinks, but as Orville didn't have any family that he knew of, he was happy to be on duty as normal.

Peter, Peggy, Hebe and Harry joined us at the gates. Normally, Hebe wore shorts and a T-shirt, but tonight she was wearing an embroidered, white, floor-length dress, and she had pinned an orange flower into her hair. On one wrist she wore a string bracelet from which dangled a little, carved wooden animal. I supposed Harry's pet monkey had made the bracelet but who had made the carving, I wondered.

This gave me an *idea*.

Hebe looked beautiful. "Pretty as a princess," I heard Harry tell her when he kissed her on the cheek. She didn't seem to mind him kissing her, in fact, she looked rather pleased about it.

Harry had also made an effort; he was wearing long trousers, clean shoes and a colourful animal print shirt. I saw Hebe put her small hand in his and gaze into his eyes. I wondered if this was the thing called 'love'. I decided to ask Grandpa about it at school on Sunday.

Peggy looked wonderful, dressed in an emerald green dress with a matching green necklace and sandals and, although Peter had put on some clean trousers, he still wore his scruffy old hat.

He told his wife that she looked beautiful and put his arm around her. This love thing was in the air, it seemed…

"Come on, everybody, we're going to start the games," he prompted.

"I'm waiting for my mother and sisters," said Little Horn longingly.

"I'm waiting for my parents," added Kili. "Solo promised he'd bring them."

"Okay, but you little ones stay inside the gates at *all* times," ordered Peter. "No wandering outside: there are snakes and scorpions out there."

My name is Happiness

"I'll keep an eye on them with Buffy and Orville," I promised.

We could hear the party was in full swing, the band were playing wonderful bing-bong music and everyone was chatting and laughing, but Kili and Little Horn would not leave the gate – *their* families still hadn't come.

Buffy and I waited patiently with them, and soon a couple of buffalo strolled up to the gate.

"Crikey, I don't believe it!" gasped Buffy. "If it isn't my brother and sister!" They didn't speak as they walked past him; they just nodded at him sullenly.

"Even Buffy's family have come," whispered Kili to Little Horn. "What happens if nobody comes for us and we can never go home?" Sobs shook her young shoulders as huge tears dripped off the end of her trunk.

"I think I'd better take her inside and distract her," suggested Buffy, but just as he was starting to lead her away, three dark outlines came into view, swaying slowly towards us.

Within moments their huge silhouettes were unmistakable.

"Mama! Papa! Uncle Solo!" Kili cried as she ran towards them, tripping over her trunk and somersaulting onto her father's foot.

Scooping her up, her father placed her in the bend of her mother's trunk, where she swung happily. He planted kisses on her painted skin, blew air softly into her trunk and wiped away her tears. Her eyes shone with joy and her cheeks flushed pink.

"Mama, Mama, I'm so happy!" she trumpeted from her safe swing. Little Horn watched on enviously.

Kili's father spoke first: "I can't thank you enough for what you did yesterday, little Happiness; you have made the reserve a safer place, reunited Solo into the herd and cared for our baby. We will be indebted to you for the rest of our lives."

Then Kili's mother spoke, so very softly for such a giant. "We feared we might never see our daughter again. She could have died from thirst or been taken by a lion. This is the happiest day of my life."

"It was Peter and Harry who saved her, all we've done is be friends with her until you came. Please, do go in to the party and join in the fun."

"You're a little champ, Happiness. I'll be on your team anytime."

"Thanks, Solo. I think you're very brave and I'd like you on my team!"

The elephants took turns to stroke my cheeks with their trunks and gently planted elephant kisses on my head. I turned to watch them walk majestically towards the sound of the music but when I turned back, a split second later, I noticed with absolute horror that Little Horn was missing. My mind went into a complete spin: he must have wandered outside the gates and was nowhere to be seen. Thankfully, Orville was circling above my head.

"Hey!" I snorted as loudly as I could. "Little Horn's gone missing!"

"I don't know how he got past me but he can't have gone far," he said in a calm voice, although I could sense he was panicking. We both knew that the snakes or scorpions that hadn't been invited would be happy to kill one of our guests out of sweet revenge.

My name is Happiness

I also knew I should tell Peter and Harry, but there just wasn't time to do so. Buffy had been preoccupied with directing guests to different parts of the garden and also hadn't noticed Little Horn's escape.

"Buffy, I think Little Horn has gone out to look for his mother; I must go and find him."

"Not without me, you don't," replied the buffalo. "Mango, the guests are all here now so close the gates and say nothing to anyone. We'll be back as soon as we can."

We followed Little Horn's footprints and scent easily. We knew he would be safe for the time being because Orville was dive-bombing and screeching at anything suspicious.

Thankfully, after what felt like forever, we found him sitting alone with his eyes squeezed tightly shut and a small pool of tears at his feet. His birthday hankie was missing from his neck, and he was concentrating so hard that he didn't hear our approach.

Little Horn on hankie

"Little Horn," I said softly. "What on *earth* are you doing?"

He almost jumped out of his skin. "Oh, it's you, Happy. I'm sitting on my lucky charm and wishing for my mother to come. This is where my father died, you see, right on this spot."

He stood up and showed me the flattened hankie. "I couldn't stand it any longer. I don't know where my mother and sisters are; maybe they've been shot too. I just had to come here and make a wish on my lucky charm."

"Can I wish with you?" I asked.

"Yes, please. Wish really hard," replied Little Horn.

Dear old Buffy stood over us, keeping a lookout as we wished and wished.

"Please, let me see my family again; please, make them safe," whispered Little Horn, over and over again.

"Goodness me, look who's here," interrupted Buffy, sounding surprised.

"Hey, man, what are you doing here?"

Zulu had appeared silently out of nowhere and Orville swooped down from the sky and landed silently on Buffy's back.

"Buffy old boy, I've got a little birthday surprise for Little Horn," purred Zulu. "There's someone coming to see you."

Little Horn frowned. "Who could that be?"

Orville winked and looked over his shoulder. The sound of heavy footsteps hurried towards us in a cloud of dust.

The dust settled and Little Horn gasped. "Mummy, is it really you?"

"Yes, my baby boy, it really is me and your sisters too,"

replied his mother. She rubbed her head against his side as his sisters touched noses with him in turn. The mother rhino was enormous but so tender with him.

"Hello, Dusty. Hello, Nosy." Little Horn pressed his nose back against theirs.

"Hello, Little Horn," said the twins, "we've been very worried about you and we miss Daddy so much." The babies started to weep and Buffy turned his head away from the touching scene, but not before I saw the tears well up in his eyes.

"It's just wonderful to see you again, my pet, and happy birthday, darling!"

"Is it really my birthday today, Mummy?"

"Umm, I not sure, but rhinos can choose any day they like."

"Can it be ours too, then?" chorused Dusty and Nosy.

"I don't see why not," agreed Buffy.

"I heard about the party but I was scared to come without your father to protect your sisters," continued the mother, "then something most unexpected happened: my new friend Zulu here came to us and offered to escort us to Weaver House and then Orville intercepted us en route and told us he'd spotted you sitting here on your own. Why, dearest, are you out here alone?"

"I didn't know what else to do except wish really hard on my lucky charm," he explained. "And I thought that if I came to the spot where Daddy died and wished really hard it might help me find you."

"My darling boy, I was always coming to fetch you once it was safe. What is your lucky charm?"

"This," he said, picking the flat hankie up between his lips, "but I don't need it any more now you've found me. And this is my new friend Happiness, she has a lucky charm too!"

"I'm very pleased to meet you, Happiness," said his mother, "but let's not stay here any longer, this place has too many sad memories."

"I agree," said Zulu. "This is a very special day, so let's go and celebrate!"

"Yes, let's. It's a bit scary here," said Little Horn.

He trotted gaily alongside his family and didn't stop talking once. His sisters hung on his every word. He told them how scared he'd been, but how his new friends had helped him cope with being away from them. He told them that he had been adopted lots and lots of times by lots of people, but only so that he could go home to his real mother one day.

His mother listened intently the whole time, not taking her eyes off him even for a second.

When we got back, Hebe was waiting anxiously at the gates with Mango. She flung her arms around Little Horn's neck. "You naughty little boy, where did you go? You must *never* go out alone!"

"I went to find my family," he replied simply. "And my lucky charm worked because here they are! This is Mummy and these are my sisters, Dusty and Nosy."

"This is the best day of my life," Hebe said, patting the little sisters. "Welcome, everyone. Please, come in and meet my family." She shouted above the noise of the band, "Attention, everyone! Look who's here!"

The band stopped playing and, when the family entered the

gardens, a huge cheer went up because *everyone knows rhinos are very special and very rare.*

"Welcome – please come in," offered Peter. "Gather round, everyone."

It took several minutes for the guests to all take their places; those that were still playing games continued to do so but others climbed trees for a better view and some youngsters balanced on their elders' shoulders. Small animals and the little five pushed to the front, while the larger ones stayed at the back.

Climbing onto a chair, Peter looked around at the party guests. "I'd like to welcome everyone, friends old and new. This is an incredible day and one that none of us will ever forget; not only have six evil poachers been caught, but Little Horn and Kili have been reunited with their families."

Another cheer went up, and Peter continued, "This is a birthday celebration and tonight you are all at peace with one another, although tomorrow some of you might quarrel or even eat each other! As rangers our battle against the poachers is very difficult, but we promise you that we will do everything we can to protect you all and with Happiness around, I think we can beat them!" Another cheer went up.

"Happiness is a hero," they chanted over and over.

Peter held up his hands, politely hushing them, and carried on. "We must educate the poachers, and try to convince them to work *for* us not against us, in return for their freedom. We also need GPS collars for the elephants and rhinos so we can track their movements. We must stop trees from being felled so that you don't lose your homes. All this needs money, which is something you animals can't provide."

"Excuse me," coughed Mango. "One of us can!" He waved his hat in the air.

"With a hat?" asked Peter, slightly bemused.

"This isn't just any old hat, Peter. This is a hat with pockets so you can't lose things. I keep pocket money and peanuts in mine."

"Very clever, Mango!"

"I'd like one," shouted someone from the crowd.

"So would I," called another.

Another huge cheer went up and dozens of guests put their hands in the air.

An exhilarated Mango counted his orders.

"I've got an idea too," I shouted above the noise.

"Another idea!" said Harry fondly. "Surely not more plans for catching poachers yet?"

"No, no – another way to make money! Hebe, please show everyone your bracelet." Hebe stretched out her arm and the little wooden carving dangled in the light for everyone to see. "You see this?" I said, nudging it with my snout.

"I carved that," said Harry.

"Well, if you make more carvings, each one being a small replica of the animals at Weaver House or our friends on the reserve, people can buy a bracelet when they adopt an animal and collect all the charms over time. Every time they wear it they will think of the animal and their friends will want one too."

"That's a brilliant idea," said Hebe.

"I'd love to be a charm," said Zizi.

"Me too," said Monty, posing.

"So would I," said Twig.

"And me," chorused Mango, Kili and Little Horn.

"Very clever, Happiness. I don't know what we would do without you!" hooted Orville. "I think I'd make a splendid charm."

"Now, everyone, please raise your glasses. Let's make a toast. To the success of Mango's hat business and Harry's Lucky Charms. May they both succeed and help save the animals *before it's too late*."

"*Before it's too late*," repeated the guests.

"Can we have prize-giving now?" asked Monty impatiently.

"What about the birthday cake?" chattered Mango.

"All you think about is your stomach, Mango!" chuckled Monty.

"Here it is, Mango!" said Peggy. She wheeled a trolley into the middle of the garden. On top rested a spectacular birthday cake covered in flickering candles. Millions of fireflies appeared in the sky above our heads and shone like tiny stars.

We gathered around the cake with our eyes on stalks. She had divided the cake into two halves: one half edible for humans and the other edible for animals. The human half was covered with dozens of miniature African animals made from marzipan. She had carefully made small trees from chocolate sticks with chocolate truffles on top, used green coconut for grass and made tiny, coloured flowers from hard icing. Our side was covered in seeds and nuts.

Little Horn, Mango, Ben, Zizi, Monty, Nosy, Dusty and I (and a few others who had decided it was their birthday too) blew the candles out as hard as we could. Everyone sang Happy Birthday at the top of their voices.

"I'm allowed chocolate," declared Mango, grabbing two chocolate trees in his hand.

The games had been a great success and all the young animals hoped for a prize. Luckily, Peter had plenty to go around. He handed out the prizes to some very overexcited individuals and soon afterwards their parents gently suggested it might be time to go home.

One by one, the guests thanked us for a wonderful evening and made their way out through the flamingos. Now their work was done, Mango invited them in to use our pond and help themselves to some fish.

Peggy had already invited all our families to stay the night.

She directed them to various sleeping quarters and I took my family with me to mine. We snuggled down together and very soon a hush fell over Weaver House. I looked at the full moon shining brightly over the reserve but I had my family with me so I didn't need to wish on it.

My parents kissed me goodnight and settled down. Winkle snuggled up against me and snuffled my face.

"It was a wonderful party, Happiness, and you're so brave to have caught those scary men."

"You can help me when you're a little bit older," I whispered back. "Nighty-night, little one. Sleep tight and mind the bugs don't bite."

"I'm so happy you're coming home tomorrow, it's just not the same without you," she said sleepily.

I didn't tell her but it was then I just *knew* that I couldn't go home.

Who Goes and Who Stays?

Next morning our close friends came round to thank us for such a lovely party and then our families decided it was time to go home. There was much snorting, nuzzling and promises to stay in touch.

"Can I come to your school on Sundays?" Kili asked my grandpa.

"Of course, and bring Little Horn."

He looked up at his mother. "Will it be safe getting there and back?"

"Zulu and I will come by and pick them up," offered Buffy. "We can wait to bring them home again too."

"Thank you very much. That is most reassuring," said Little Horn's mother.

"Come and have a swim sometime," invited Sugarsnap.

"And football!" added Hugo.

"Kili, Kili," whispered Ben, "please, can I come with you?"

"Mama, please, can Ben come and live with us?"

"If you don't mind travelling you can, because we move around a lot."

"I don't mind. I promise I'll be good."

The families turned to go, and Mango wrapped his long arms around each one in turn.

"I'm going to miss them so much," cried Hebe. Harry put his arm around her shoulder to comfort her and managed another quick kiss on her cheek.

"You've still got me. I'm staying put," said Zizi.

"Me too," said Monty.

"And us," chirruped Flo, and Orville tooted.

"We've settled in well, so we'd like to stay too, p– p– p– please," said Spike.

"What about you, Twig?" Hebe spoke slowly and carefully.

"I'd like to stay with my parents; I don't feel ready to leave home yet," he mouthed carefully.

"Come along then, dear," said Mrs Twiga. "We'll pop our heads over the fence in a few days."

"Well," said Papa. "I can't thank you all enough for taking care of our dear daughter. Say your thank-yous, Happiness, and we'll get going."

"Well," I faltered. "I was just thinking... that perhaps, I could... stay on for a bit? I could help Peter and Harry."

"Don't you think you'd be in the way?" asked Papa, sounding surprised.

"Not at all," answered Peter. "I think we could really do with her help."

"Weaver House just wouldn't be the same without her," said Mango, putting his arms around me to stop me from going.

Winkle and Quiver started to cry.

"We'll miss you," said Truffle.

"She's old enough to make her own mind up," said Mama. "She's got two families now and we can still see her every day."

My parents kissed me goodbye and I rubbed snouts with my siblings.

With that, my family left and Mango closed the gates behind them.

It felt very quiet without Little Horn and Kili, so I decided to take a mud bath to cheer myself up.

"Come on, Mango," invited Hebe, taking his hand. "We've got orders to fill!"

Harry and Peter started sweeping up the mess left over from the party when they heard a scratching sound just outside the gates.

Peter opened the gate. "What is it?" asked Harry, stopping mid-sweep.

"You'll never believe what I've got," said Peter, carefully picking up a small, round shape in his hands.

"Peggy, get the nursery ready, please, it's Pickle the pangolin."

THE END

If any of you is curious to know: Twig measured 4.3 metres tall and Hugo weighed 75 kilos, but they are both still growing.

Spike and Holly had 77 quills in their pile and Flapper fitted 163 stones into his pouch.